BOOKSHOTS

AVAILABLE NOW!

CROSS KILL

Along Came a Spider killer Gary Soneji died years ago. But Alex Cross swears he sees Soneji gun down his partner. Is his greatest enemy back from the grave?

ZOO 2

Humans are evolving into a savage new species that could save civilization—or end it. James Patterson's *Zoo* was just the beginning.

THE TRIAL

An accused killer will do anything to disrupt his own trial, including a courtroom shocker that Lindsay Boxer and the Women's Murder Club will never see coming.

LITTLE BLACK DRESS

Can a little black dress change everything? What begins as one woman's fantasy is about to go too far.

LET'S PLAY MAKE-BELIEVE

Christy and Marty just met, and it's love at first sight. Or is it? One of them is playing a dangerous game—and only one will survive.

CHASE

A man falls to his death in an apparent accident.... But why does he have the fingerprints of another man who is already dead? Detective Michael Bennett is on the case.

HUNTED

Someone is luring men from the streets to play a mysterious, high-stakes game. Former Special Forces officer David Shelley goes undercover to shut it down—but will he win?

113 MINUTES

Molly Rourke's son has been murdered. Now she'll do whatever it takes to get justice. No one should underestimate a mother's love....

$10,000,000 MARRIAGE PROPOSAL

A mysterious billboard offering $10 million to get married intrigues three single women in LA. But who is Mr. Right...and is he the perfect match for the lucky winner?

FRENCH KISS

It's hard enough to move to a new city, but now everyone French detective Luc Moncrief cares about is being killed off. Welcome to New York.

LEARNING TO RIDE

City girl Madeline Harper never wanted to love a cowboy. But rodeo king Tanner Callen might change her mind...and win her heart.

THE McCULLAGH INN IN MAINE

Chelsea O'Kane escapes to Maine to build a new life—until she runs into Jeremy Holland, an old flame....

SACKING THE QUARTERBACK

Attorney Melissa St. James wins every case. Now, when she's up against football superstar Grayson Knight, her heart is on the line, too.

THE MATING SEASON

Documentary ornithologist Sophie Castle is convinced that her heart belongs only to the birds—until she meets her gorgeous cameraman, Rigg Greensman.

UPCOMING THRILLERS
BOOK**SHOTS**

KILLER CHEF

Caleb Rooney knows how to do two things: run a food truck and solve a murder. When people suddenly start dying of food-borne illnesses, the stakes are higher than ever....

THE CHRISTMAS MYSTERY

Two stolen paintings disappear from a Park Avenue murder scene— French detective Luc Moncrief is in for a merry Christmas.

BLACK & BLUE

Detective Harry Blue is determined to take down the serial killer who's abducted several women, but her mission leads to a shocking revelation.

UPCOMING ROMANCES

James Patterson's
BOOK**SHOTS**
Flames

BODYGUARD

Special Agent Abbie Whitmore has only one task: protect Congressman Jonathan Lassiter from a violent cartel's threats. Yet she's never had to do it while falling in love....

DAZZLING: THE DIAMOND TRILOGY, PART I

To support her artistic career, Siobhan Dempsey works at the elite Stone Room in New York City...never expecting to be swept away by Derick Miller.

RADIANT: THE DIAMOND TRILOGY, PART II

After an explosive breakup with her billionaire boyfriend, Siobhan moves to Detroit to pursue her art. But Derick isn't ready to give her up.

HOT WINTER NIGHTS

Allie Thatcher moved to Montana to start fresh as the head of the trauma center. And even though the days are cold, the nights are steamy... especially when she meets search-and-rescue leader Dex Belmont.

"ALEX CROSS, I'M COMING FOR YOU...."

Gary Soneji, the killer from *Along Came a Spider,* has been dead for more than ten years—but Cross swears he saw Soneji gun down his partner. Is Cross's worst enemy back from the grave?

Nothing will prepare you for the wicked truth.

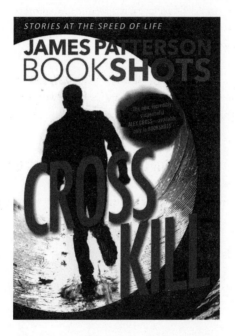

Read the next riveting, pulse-racing Alex Cross adventure, available now only from

BOOK**SHOTS**

FRENCH KISS

A DETECTIVE LUC MONCRIEF STORY

JAMES PATTERSON
WITH RICHARD DiLALLO

BOOK**SHOTS**

Little, Brown and Company
New York Boston London

Copyright © 2016 by James Patterson

BookShots / Little, Brown and Company
Hachette Book Group
1290 Avenue of the Americas, New York, NY 10104
bookshots.com

First Edition: October 2016

BookShots is an imprint of Little, Brown and Company, a division of Hachette Book Group, Inc. The Little, Brown name and logo are trademarks of Hachette Book Group, Inc. The BookShots name and logo are trademarks of JBP Business, LLC.

The publisher is not responsible for websites (or their content) that are not owned by the publisher.

The Hachette Speakers Bureau provides a wide range of authors for speaking events. To find out more, go to hachettespeakersbureau.com or call (866) 376-6591.

ISBN 978-0-316-35887-3
LCCN: 2016935244

10 9 8 7 6 5 4 3 2

LSC-C

Printed in the United States of America

FRENCH KISS

CHAPTER 1

THE WEATHERMAN NAILED IT. "Sticky, hot, and miserable. Highs in the nineties. Stay inside if you can."

I can't. I have to get someplace. Fast.

Jesus Christ, it's hot. Especially if you're running as fast as you can through Central Park *and* you're wearing a dark gray Armani silk suit, a light gray Canali silk shirt, and black Ferragamo shoes.

As you might have guessed, I am late—very, very late. *Très en retard,* as we say in France.

I pick up speed until my legs hurt. I can feel little blisters forming on my toes and heels.

Why did I ever come to New York?

Why, oh why, did I leave Paris?

If I were running like this in Paris, I would be stopping all traffic. I would be the center of attention. Men and women would be shouting for the police.

"A young businessman has gone berserk! He is shoving baby carriages out of his path. He is frightening the old ladies walking their dogs."

But this is not Paris. This is New York.

So forget it. Even the craziest event in New York goes unnoticed. The dog walkers keep on walking their dogs. The teenage lovers kiss. A toddler points to me. His mother glances up. Then she shrugs.

Will even one New Yorker dial 911? Or 311?

Forget about that also. You see, I am part of the police. A French detective now working with the Seventeenth Precinct on my specialty—drug smuggling, drug sales, and drug-related homicides.

My talent for being late has, in a mere two months, become almost legendary with my colleagues in the precinct house. But… oh, *merde*…showing up late for today's meticulously planned stakeout on Madison Avenue and 71st Street will do nothing to help my reputation, a reputation as an uncooperative rich French kid, a rebel with too many causes.

Merde…today of all days I should have known better than to wake my gorgeous girlfriend to say good-bye.

"I cannot be late for this one, Dalia."

"Just one more good-bye squeeze. What if you're shot and I never see you again?"

The good-bye "squeeze" turned out to be significantly longer than I had planned.

Eh. It doesn't matter. I'm where I'm supposed to be now. A mere forty-five minutes late.

CHAPTER 2

MY PARTNER, DETECTIVE Maria Martinez, is seated on the driver's side of an unmarked police car at 71st Street and Madison Avenue.

While keeping her eyes on the surrounding area, Maria unlocks the passenger door. I slide in, drowning in perspiration. She glances at me for a second, then speaks.

"Man. What's the deal? Did you put your suit on first and *then* take your shower?"

"Funny," I say. "Sorry I'm late."

"You should have little business cards with that phrase on it— 'Sorry I'm late.'"

I'm certain that Maria Martinez doesn't care whether I'm late. Unlike a lot of my detective colleagues, she doesn't mind that I'm not big on "protocol." I'm late a lot. I do a lot of careless things. I bring ammo for a Glock 22 when I'm packing a Glock 27. I like a glass or two of white wine with lunch…it's a long list. But Maria overlooks most of it.

My other idiosyncrasies she has come to accept, more or less. I must have a proper *déjeuner.* That's lunch. No mere sandwich will do. What's more, a glass or two of good wine never did anything but enhance the flavor of a lunch.

You see, Maria "gets" me. Even better, she knows what I know:

together we're a cool combination of her procedure-driven methods and my purely instinct-driven methods.

"So where are we with this bust?" I say.

"We're still sitting on our butts. That's where we are," she says. Then she gives details.

"They got two pairs of cops on the other side of the street, and two other detectives—Imani Williams and Henry Whatever-the-Hell-His-Long-Polish-Name-Is—at the end of the block. That team'll go into the garage.

"Then there's another team behind the garage. They'll hold back and *then* go into the garage.

"Then they got three guys on the roof of the target building."

The target building is a large former town house that's now home to a store called Taylor Antiquities. It's a place filled with the fancy antique pieces lusted after by trust-fund babies and hedge-fund hotshots. Maria and I have already cased Taylor Antiquities a few times. It's a store where you can lay down your Amex Centurion card and walk away with a white jade vase from the Yuan dynasty or purchase the four-poster bed where John and Abigail Adams reportedly conceived little John Quincy.

"And what about us?"

"Our assignment spot is inside the store," she says.

"No. I want to be where the action is," I say.

"Be careful what you wish for," Maria says. "Do what they tell you. We're inside the store. Over and out. Meanwhile, how about watching the street with me?"

Maria Martinez is total cop. At the moment she is heart-and-soul into the surveillance. Her eyes dart from the east side of the street to the west. Every few seconds, she glances into the rearview mirror. Follows it with a quick look into the side-view mirror. Searches straight ahead. Then she does it all over again.

Me? Well, I'm looking around, but I'm also wondering if I can take a minute off to grab a cardboard cup of lousy American coffee.

Don't get me wrong. And don't be put off by what I said about my impatience with "procedure." No. I am very cool with being a detective. In fact, I've wanted to be a detective since I was four years old. I'm also very good at my job. And I've got the résumé to prove it.

Last year in Pigalle, one of the roughest parts of Paris, I solved a drug-related gang homicide and made three on-the-scene arrests. Just me and a twenty-five-year-old traffic cop.

I was happy. I was successful. For a few days I was even famous.

The next morning the name Luc Moncrief was all over the newspapers and the Internet. A rough translation of the headline on the front page of *Le Monde*:

OLDEST PIGALLE DRUG GANG SMASHED BY YOUNGEST PARIS DETECTIVE— LUC MONCRIEF

Underneath was this subhead:

Parisian Heartthrob Hauls in Pigalle Drug Lords

The paparazzi had always been somewhat interested in whom I was dating; after that, they were obsessed. Club owners comped my table with bottles of Perrier-Jouët Champagne. Even my father, the chairman of a giant pharmaceuticals company, gave me one of his rare compliments.

"Very nice job…for a playboy. Now I hope you've got this 'detective thing' out of your system."

I told him thank you, but I did not tell him that "this detective thing" was not out of my system. Or that I enjoyed the very generous monthly allowance that he gave me too much.

So when my *capitaine supérieur* announced that the NYPD wanted to trade one of their art-forgery detectives for one of our Paris drug enforcement detectives for a few months, I jumped at the offer. From my point of view, it was a chance to reconnect with my former lover, Dalia Boaz. From my Parisian *lieutenant* point of view, it was an opportunity to add some needed discipline and learning to my instinctive approach to detective work.

So here I am. On Madison Avenue, my eyes are burning with sweat. I can actually feel the perspiration squishing around in my shoes.

Detective Martinez remains focused completely on the street scene. But God, I need some coffee, some air. I begin speaking.

"Listen. If I could just jump out for a minute and—"

As I'm about to finish the sentence, two vans—one black, one red—turn into the garage next door to Taylor Antiquities.

Our cell phones automatically buzz with a loud sirenlike sound. The doors of the unmarked police cars begin to open.

As Maria and I hit the street, she speaks.

"It looks like our evidence has finally arrived."

CHAPTER 3

MARTINEZ AND I RUSH into Taylor Antiquities. There are no customers. A skinny middle-aged guy sits at a desk in the rear of the store, and a typical debutante—a young blond woman in a white linen skirt and a black shirt—is dusting some small, silver-topped jars.

It is immediately clear to both of them that we're not here to buy an ancient Thai penholder. We are easily identified as two very unpleasant-looking cops, the male foolishly dressed in an expensive waterlogged suit, the woman in too-tight khaki pants. Maria and I are each holding our NYPD IDs in our left hands and our pistols in our right hands.

"You. Freeze!" Maria shouts at the blond woman.

I yell the same thing at the guy at the desk.

"You freeze, too, sir," I say.

From our two pre-bust surveillance visits I recognize the man as Blaise Ansel, the owner of Taylor Antiquities.

Ansel begins walking toward us.

I yell again. "I said freeze, Mr. Ansel. This…is…a…drug…raid."

"This is police-department madness," Ansel says, and now he is almost next to us. The debutante hasn't moved a muscle.

"Cuff him, Luc. He's resisting." Maria is pissed.

Ansel throws his hands into the air. "No. No. I am not resisting anything but the intrusion. I *am* freezing. Look."

Although I have seen him before, I have never heard him speak. His accent is foreign, thick. It's an accent that's easy for anyone to identify. Ansel is a Frenchman. Son of a bitch. One of ours.

As Ansel freezes, three patrol cars, lights flashing, pull up in front of the store. Then I tell the young woman to join us. She doesn't move. She doesn't speak.

"Please join us," Maria says. Now the woman moves to us. Slowly. Cautiously.

"Your name, ma'am?" I ask.

"Monica Ansel," she replies.

Blaise Ansel looks at Martinez and me.

"She's my wife."

There's got to be a twenty-year age difference between the two of them, but Maria and I remain stone-faced. Maria taps on her cell phone and begins reading aloud from the screen.

"To make this clear: we are conducting a drug search based on probable cause. Premises and connected premises are 861 Madison Avenue, New York, New York, in the borough of Manhattan, June 21, 2016. Premises title: Taylor Antiquities, Inc. Chairman and owner: Blaise Martin Ansel. Company president: Blaise Martin Ansel."

Maria taps the screen and pushes another button.

"This is being recorded," she says.

I would never have read the order to search, but Maria is strictly by the book.

"This is preposterous," says Blaise Ansel.

Maria does not address Ansel's comment. She simply says, "I want you to know that detectives and officers are currently positioned in your delivery dock, your garage, and your rooftop. They will be interviewing all parties of interest. It is our assignment to interview both you and the woman you've identified as your wife."

"Drugs? Are you mad?" yells Ansel. "This shop is a museum-quality repository of rare antiques. Look. Look."

Ansel quickly moves to one of the display tables. He holds up a carved mahogany box. "A fifteenth-century tea chest," he says. He lifts the lid of the box. "What do you see inside? Cocaine? Heroin? Marijuana?"

It is obvious that Maria has decided to allow Ansel to continue his slightly crazed demonstration.

"This—this, too," Ansel says as he moves to a pine trunk set on four spindly legs. "An American colonial sugar safe. Nothing inside. No crystal meth, no sugar."

Ansel is about to present two painted Chinese-looking bowls when the rear entrance to the shop opens and Imani Williams enters. Detective Williams is agitated. She is also *très belle*.

"Not a damn thing in those two vans," she says. "Police mechanics are searching the undersides, but there's nothing but a bunch of empty gold cigarette boxes and twelve Iranian silk rugs in the cargo. We tested for drug traces. They all came up negative."

I think I catch an exchange of glances between Monsieur and

Madame Ansel. I *think*. I'm not sure. But the more I think, well, the more sure I become.

"Detective Williams," I say. "Do you think you could fill in for me for a few minutes to assist Detective Martinez with the Ansel interview?"

"Yeah, sure," says Williams. "Where you going?"

"I just need to…I'm not sure…look around."

"Tell the truth, Moncrief. You've been craving a cup of joe since you got here," says Maria Martinez.

"Can't fool you, partner," I say.

I open the shop door. I'm out.

CHAPTER 4

THE SUFFOCATING AIR ON Madison Avenue almost shimmers with heat.

Where have all the beautiful people gone? East Hampton? Bar Harbor? The South of France?

I walk the block. I watch a man polish the handrail alongside the steps of Saint James' Church. I see the tourists line up outside Ladurée, the French *macaron* store.

A young African American man, maybe eighteen years old, walks near me. He is bare-chested. He seems even sweatier than I am. The young man's T-shirt is tied around his neck, and he is guzzling from a quart-size bottle of water.

"Where'd you get that?" I ask.

"A dude like you can go to that fancy-ass cookie store. You got five bills, that'll get you a soda there," he says.

"But where'd you get *that* bottle, the water you're drinking?" I ask again.

"Us poor bros go to Kenny's. You're practically in it right now."

He gestures toward 71st Street between Madison and Park Avenues. As the kid moves away, I figure that the "fancy-ass cookie store" is Ladurée. I am equidistant between a five-dollar soda and a cheaper but larger bottle of water. Why waste Papa's generous allowance on fancy-ass soda?

Kenny's is a tiny storefront, a place you should find closer to Ninth Avenue than Madison Avenue. Behind the counter is a Middle Eastern-type guy. Kenny? He peddles only newspapers, cigarettes, lottery tickets, and, for some reason, Dial soap.

I examine the contents of Kenny's small refrigerated case. It holds many bottles, all of them the same—the no-name water that the shirtless young man was drinking. At the moment that water looks to me like heaven in a bottle.

"I'm going to take two of these bottles," I say.

"One second, please, sir," says the man behind the counter, then he addresses another man who is wheeling four brown cartons of candy into the store. The cartons are printed with the name and logo for Snickers. The man steering the dolly looks very much like the counterman. Is he Kenny? Is anybody Kenny? I consider buying a Snickers bar. No. The wet Armani suit is already growing tighter.

"How many more boxes are there, Hector?" the counterman asks.

"At least fifteen more," comes the response. Then "Kenny" turns to me.

"And you, sir?" the counterman asks.

"No. Nothing," I say. "Sorry."

I leave the tiny store and break into a run. I am around the corner on Madison Avenue. I punch the button on my phone marked 4. Direct connection to Martinez. All I can think is: *What the hell? Twenty cartons of candy stored in a shop the size of a closet? Twenty cartons of Snickers in a store that doesn't even sell candy?*

She answers and starts talking immediately. "Williams and I are getting nowhere with these two assholes. This whole thing sucks. Our intelligence is all screwed up. There's nothing here."

I am only slightly breathless, only slightly nervous.

"Listen to me. It's all here, where I am. I know it."

"What the hell are you talking about?" she says.

"A newsstand between Madison and Park. Kenny's. I'm less than two hundred feet away from you guys. Leave one person at Taylor Antiquities and get everyone over here. Now."

"How—?"

"The two vans, the garage…that's all a decoy," I say. "The real shit is being unloaded here…in cartons of candy bars."

"How do you know?"

"Like the case in Pigalle. *I know because I know.*"

CHAPTER 5

ONE MONTH LATER. IT'S another sweltering summer day in Manhattan.

A year ago I was working in the detective room at the precinct on rue Achille-Martinet in Paris. Today I'm working in the detective room at the precinct on East 51st Street in Manhattan.

But the crime is absolutely the same. In both cities, men, women, and children sell drugs, kill for drugs, and all too often die for drugs.

My desk faces Maria Martinez's scruffy desk. She's not in yet. Uh-oh. She may be picking up my bad habits. *Pas possible*. Not Maria.

I drink my coffee and begin reading the blotter reports of last night's arrests. No murders, no drug busts. So much for interesting blotter reports.

I call my coolest, hippest, chicest New York contact—Patrick, one of the doormen at 15 Central Park West, where I live with Dalia. Patrick is trying to score me a dinner reservation at Rao's, the impossible-to-get-into restaurant in East Harlem.

Merde. I am on my cell phone when my boss, Inspector Nick Elliott, the chief inspector for my division, stops by. I hold up my "just a minute" index finger. Since the Taylor Antiquities drug bust I have a little money in the bank with my boss, but it won't last forever, and this hand gesture certainly won't help.

At last I sigh. No tables. Maybe next month. When I hang up the phone I say, "I'm sorry, Inspector. I was just negotiating a favor with a friend who might be able to score me a table at Rao's next week."

Elliott scowls and says, "Far be it from me to interrupt your off-duty life, Moncrief, but you may have noticed that your partner isn't at her desk."

"I noticed. Don't forget, I'm a detective."

He ignores my little joke.

"In case you're wondering, Detective Martinez is on loan to Vice for two days."

"Why didn't you or Detective Martinez tell me this earlier? You must have known before today."

"Yeah, I knew about it yesterday, but I told Martinez to hold off telling you. That it would just piss you off to be left out, and I was in no rush to listen to you get pissed off," Elliott says.

"So why *wasn't* I included?" I ask.

"You weren't necessary. They just needed a woman. Though I don't owe you any explanations about assignments."

The detective room has grown quieter. I'm sure that a few of my colleagues—especially the men—are enjoying seeing Elliott put me in my place.

Fact is, I like Elliott; he's a pretty straight-arrow guy, but I have been developing a small case of paranoia about being excluded from hot assignments.

"What can Maria do that I can't do?" I ask.

"If you can't answer that, then that pretty-boy face of yours isn't doing you much good," Elliott says with a laugh. Then his tone of voice turns serious.

"Anyway, we got something going on up the road a piece. They got a situation at Brioni. That's a fancy men's store just off Fifth Avenue. Get a squad car driver to take you there. Right now."

"Which Brioni?" I ask.

"I just told you—Brioni on Fifth Avenue."

"There are *two* Brionis: 57 East 57th Street and 55 East 52nd Street," I say.

Elliott begins to walk away. He stops. He turns to me. He speaks.

"You *would* know something like that."

CHAPTER 6

WHAT'S THE ONE QUESTION that's guaranteed to piss off any New York City detective or cop?

"Don't you guys have anything better to do with your time?"

If you're a cop who's ever ticketed someone for running a red light; if you're a detective who's ever asked a mother why her child wasn't in school that day, then you've heard it.

I enter the Brioni store, at 57 East 57th Street. My ego is bruised, and my mood is lousy. Frankly, I am usually in Brioni as a customer, not a policeman. Plus, is there nothing more humiliating than an eager detective sent to investigate a shoplifting crime?

I'm in an even lousier mood when the first thing I'm asked is, "Don't you guys have anything better to do with your time?" The suspect doesn't ask this question. No. It comes from one of the arresting officers, a skinny young African American guy who is at the moment cuffing a young African American kid. The minor has been nabbed by store security. He was trying to lift three cashmere sweaters, and now the kid is scared as shit.

"You should know better than to ask that question," I say to the cop. "Meanwhile, take the cuffs off the kid."

The cop does as he's told, but he clearly does not know when to shut up. So he speaks.

"Sorry, Detective. I just meant that it's pretty unusual to send a detective out on an arrest that's so...so..."

He is searching for a word, and I supply it. "Unimportant."

"Yeah, that's it," the young officer says. "Unimportant."

The officer now realizes that the subject is closed. He gives me some details. The kid, age twelve, was brought in for petty robbery this past February. But I'm only half listening. I'm pissed off, and I'm pissed off because the cop is right—it's unimportant. This case is incredibly unimportant, laughably unimportant. It's ridiculous to be sent on such a stupid little errand. Other NYPD detectives are unraveling terrorist plots, going undercover to frame mob bosses. Me, I'm overseeing the arrest of a little kid who stole three cashmere sweaters.

As Maria Martinez has often said to me, "Someone with your handsome face and your expensive suit shouldn't be sent on anything but the most important assignments." Then she'd laugh, and I would stare at her in stony silence...until I also laughed.

"We have the merch all bagged," says the other officer. The name Callahan is on his nameplate. Callahan is a guy with very pink cheeks and an even pinker nose. He looks maybe thirty-five or forty...or whatever age a cop is when he's smart enough not to ask "Don't you have anything better to do with your time?"

"Thanks," I say.

But what I'm really thinking about is: *Who the hell gave me this nauseatingly* petite *assignment?*

I'm sure it's not Elliott. Ah, *oui,* the inspector and I aren't exactly what they call best buds, but he's grown used to me. He thinks he's being funny when he calls me Pretty Boy, but he also trusts me, and, like almost everyone else, he's very pleased with the bust I (almost single-handedly) helped pull off at Taylor Antiquities.

I know that my partner, Maria Martinez, puts out good press on me. As I've said, she and I are simpatico, to say the least. I like her. She likes me. Case closed.

Beyond that, anyone higher than Elliott doesn't know I exist. So I can't assume that one of the assistant commissioners or one of the ADAs is out to get me.

"There's a squad car outside to bring him in," Callahan says.

"Hold on a minute. I want to talk to the kid," I say.

I walk over to the boy. He wears jeans cut off at midcalf, very clean white high-top sneakers, and an equally clean white T-shirt. It's a look I could live without.

"Why'd you try to steal three sweaters? It's the goddamn middle of summer, and you're stealing sweaters. Are you stupid?"

I can tell that if he starts talking he's going to cry.

No answer. He looks away. At the ceiling. At the floor. At the young cop and Callahan.

"How old are you?" I ask.

"Sixteen," he says. My instinct was right. He does start to cry. He squints hard, trying to stem the flow of tears.

"You're a lousy liar *and* a lousy thief. You're twelve. You're in the system. Don't you think the officers checked? You were picked up five months ago. You and a friend tried to hold up a liquor store on East Tremont. They got you then, too. You *are* stupid."

The kid shouts at me. No tears now.

"I ain't stupid. I kinda thought they'd have a buzzer or some shit in the liquor store. And I kinda felt that fat-ass guy here with the ugly-mother brown shoes was a security guy. But I don't know. Both times I decided to try it. I decided…I'm not sure why."

"Listen. Good advice number one. Kids who are assholes turn into grown-ups who are assholes.

"Good advice number two. If you've got smart instincts, *follow them*. You know what? Forget good advice. You've got a feeling? Go with it."

He sort of nods in agreement. So I keep talking.

"Look, asshole. This advice is life advice. I'm not trying to teach you how to be a better thief. I'm just trying to…oh, shit…I don't know what I'm trying to teach you."

A pause. The kid looks down at the floor so intensely that I have to look down there myself. Nothing's there but gray carpet squares.

Then the kid looks at me. He speaks.

"I get you, man," he says.

"Good." A pause. "Now go home. You've got a home?"

"I got a home. I got a grandma."

"Then go."

"What the fu—?"

"Just go."

He runs to the door.

The young officer looks at me. Then he says, "That's just great. They send a detective to the scene. And he lets the suspect go."

I don't smile. I don't answer. I walk to a nearby table where beautiful silk ties and pocket squares are laid out in groups according to color. I focus on the yellow section—yellow with blue stripes, yellow with tiny red dots, yellow paisley, yellow…

My cell phone pings. The message on the screen is big and bold and simple. CD. Cop Down.

No details. Just an address: 655 Park Avenue. Right now.

CHAPTER 7

COPS AND LIGHTS AND miles of yellow tape: POLICE LINE DO NOT CROSS.

Sirens and detectives crowd the blocks between 65th and 67th Streets. Even the mayor's car (license NYC 1) is here.

People from the neighborhood, doormen on break, and students from Hunter College try to catch a glimpse of the scene. Hundreds of people stand on the blocked-off avenue. It's a tragedy and a block party at the same time.

Detective Gabriel Ruggie approaches me. There will be no French-guy jokes, no late-guy jokes, no Pretty Boy jokes. This is serious shit. Ruggie talks.

"Elliott is up there now. The scene is at the seventh floor front. He said to send you up right away."

I walk through the fancy lobby. It's loaded with cops and reporters and detectives. I hear a brief litany of somber "hellos" and "hiyas," most of them followed by various mispronunciations of my name.

Luke. Look. Luck.

Who the hell cares now? This is Cop Down.

Detective Christine Liang is running the elevator along with a plainclothes officer.

"Hey, Moncrief. Let me take you up," Liang says. "The inspector's been asking where you are."

What the hell is the deal? Ten minutes ago I'm supervising New York's dumbest little crime of the day. Now, all of a sudden, the most serious type of crime—officer homicide—requires my attention.

"Good—you're here," Elliott says as I step from the elevator. I feel as if he's been waiting for me. It's the typical chaos of a homicide, with fingerprinting people, computer people, the coroner's people—all the people who are really smart, really thorough; but honestly, none of them ever seem to come up with information that helps solve the case.

I'm scared. I don't mind saying it. Elliott hits his phone and says, "Moncrief is here now."

"Who's that?" I ask.

"Just headquarters. I let them know you were here. They were trying to track you down."

"But you knew where I was. You sent me there," I say, confused.

"Yeah, I know. I know." Elliott seems confused, too.

"What's the deal?" I ask.

"Come with me," Elliott says. The crowd of NYPD people parts for us as if we're celebrities. We walk down a wide hall with black and white marble squares on the floor, two real Warhols on the walls. Suddenly I have a flash of an apartment in Paris—the high ceilings, the carved cornices. But in a moment I've traveled back from boulevard Haussmann to Park Avenue.

At the end of the hallway, an officer stands in front of an open door. Bright lights—floodlights, examination lights—pour from the room into the hallway. The officer moves aside immediately as Elliott and I approach.

Three people are huddled in a group near a window. I catch sight of a body, a woman. Elliott and I walk toward the group. We are still a few feet away when I see her. When my heart leaps up.

Maria Martinez.

A black plastic sheet covers her torso. Her head, blood speckling and staining her hair, is exposed.

Elliott puts a hand on my shoulder. I don't yell or cry or shake. A numbness shoots through me, and then the words tumble out.

"How? How?"

"I told you this morning, she was on loan to Vice. They had her playing the part of a high-class call girl. It seems that...well, whoever she was supposed to meet decided to...well, take a knife to her stomach."

I say nothing. I keep staring at my dead partner. Elliott decides to fill the air with words. I know he means well.

"The owners of this place are at their house in Nantucket. No servants were home...no..."

I've stopped listening. Elliott stops talking. The police photographers keep clicking away. Phil Namanworth, the coroner, is typing furiously on his laptop. Cops and detectives come and go.

Maria is dead. She looks so peaceful. Isn't that what people always say? But it's true. At least in this case it's true. In death there is peace, but there's no peace for those of us left behind.

Elliott looks me straight in the eye.

"Ya know, Moncrief, I'd like to say that in time you'll get over this." He pauses. "But I'd be a liar."

"And a good cop never lies," I say softly.

"Come back to the precinct in my car," Elliott says.

"No, thank you," I answer. "There's someplace I've got to be."

CHAPTER 8

IT'S THE SOUTHWEST CORNER of 177th Street and Fort Washington Avenue. Maria and Joey Martinez's building. I had never been there before, although Maria kept insisting that Dalia and I had to come by some night for "crazy chicken and rice," her mother's recipe.

"You'll taste it, you'll love it, and you won't be able to guess the secret ingredient," she would say.

But we never set a date, and now I am about to visit her apartment while two cops are standing guard outside the building and two detectives are inside questioning neighbors. I was her partner. I've got to see Maria's family.

A short pudgy man opens the apartment door. The living room is noisy, packed. People are crying, yelling, speaking Spanish and English. The big window air conditioner is noisy.

"I'm Maria's brother-in-law," says the man at the door.

"I'm Maria's partner from work," I say.

His face shows no expression. He nods, then says, "Joey and me are about to go downtown. They wouldn't let him—the husband, the actual husband—go to the crime scene. Now they'll let us go see her. In the morgue."

A handsome young Latino man walks quickly toward me. It has

to be Joey Martinez. He is nervous, animated, red-eyed. He grabs me firmly by the shoulders. The room turns silent, like somebody turned an Off switch.

"You're Moncrief. I know you from your pictures. Maria has a million pictures of you on her phone," he says.

"Yeah," I say. "She loves clicking away on that cell phone."

I can't help but notice that he calls me by my last name. I don't know why. Maybe that's how Maria referred to me at home.

I try to move closer to give Joey a hug. But he moves back, blocking any sort of embrace. So I speak.

"I don't know what to say, Joey. This is an incredible tragedy. Your heart must be breaking. I'm so sorry."

"Your heart must be breaking also," Joey says.

"It is," I say. "Maria was the best partner a detective could hope for. Smart. Patient. Tough…" Joey may not be weeping, but I feel myself choking up.

Joey gestures to his brother. It's a "Let's go" toss of his head.

"Look, my brother and I are going down to see Maria. But Moncrief…"

There's that last-name-only thing again. "I need to ask you something."

Now I'm nervous, but I'm not at all sure why. Something is off. The room remains silent. Brother is now standing next to brother.

"Sure," I say. "Ask me. Ask me anything."

Joey Martinez's sad and empty eyes widen. He looks directly at me and speaks slowly. "How do you have the nerve to come to my house?"

I feel confusion, and I'm sure that my face is communicating it. "Because I feel so terrible, so awful, so sad. Maria was my partner. We spent hours and hours together."

Joey continues speaking at the same slow pace. "Yes. I know. Maria loved you."

"And I loved her," I say.

"You don't understand. Or you're a liar. Maria *loved* you. She really loved you."

His words are so crazy and so untrue that I have no idea how to respond. "Joey. Please. You're experiencing a tragedy. You're totally…well…you're totally wrong about Maria, about me."

"She told me," he says. "It's not a misunderstanding. She didn't mean you were just good friends. We talked about it a thousand times. She *loved* you."

Now he pushes his face close to mine. "You think because you're rich and good-looking you can get whatever you want. You think—"

"Joey. Wait. This is insane!" I shout.

He shouts even louder. "Stop it! Just shut up. Just leave!" He shakes his head. The tears are coming fast. "My brother and I gotta go."

CHAPTER 9

WHEN I GET HOME, Dalia is waiting for me in the apartment foyer. Her hug is strong. Her kiss is soft—not sexual per se—just the perfect gentle touch of warmth. The tenderness of Dalia's kiss immediately signals to me that she's already heard about Maria Martinez's death. I'm not surprised. The DA's office has access to all NYPD information, and Dalia knows her way around her job.

Dalia is an ADA for Manhattan district attorney Fletcher Sinclair. She heads up the investigation division. The two qualities that the job requires—brains and persistence—are the two qualities Dalia seems to have in endless supply. Nothing and no one stands in her way when she's hot on an investigation.

Every day at work she tones down her tall and skinny fashion-model look with a ponytail, sensible skirts, and almost no makeup. When Dalia's at her job, she's all about the job. Laser-focused. Don't mess with the ADA.

Some evenings, when Dalia's dressed for some ultrachic charity dinner, even I have a hard time believing that this breathtakingly *belle* woman in her Georgina Chapman gown is one of the toughest lawyers in New York City.

"We got word about Maria at the DA's office late this morning," she says. "I was going to call or text or something, but I didn't want to butt in. I didn't want to nudge you if you didn't need me...."

"You can always nudge me, because I always need you," I say.

"I opened a nice Chilean Chardonnay. You want a glass and we can talk?" she asks.

"Yes," I say. "Mix a glass of wine with a quart of tequila and we'll have a drink that *might* make me forget what a miserable day this has been."

"Maria, Maria, Maria," Dalia says. She shakes her head as she pours the wine into two wineglasses. Then she says, "I hate to ask, but...any ideas yet?"

"I sure don't have any guesses. I don't even have all the details yet. Plus Maria's husband is a crazy mess right now." I decide to skip the details.

"Understandably," Dalia says.

I cannot shake the mental picture of Joey Martinez's hurt and anger as he spat out the words "She *loved* you."

Then Dalia says, "But what about you? How are you feeling?"

"How *can* I feel? Maria was my partner, and she was as good a partner as anyone ever had. She was damn near perfect. As my rugby coach used to say, 'The best combination for any job is the brains of an owl and the skin of an elephant.'"

"What was the name of the genius who came up with that little saying?" Dalia asks.

"Monsieur Pierre LeBec. You must remember him—the fat little man who was always smoking a pipe. He coached boys' rugby and taught geometry," I say. A reminiscence is about to open up.

Dalia and I speak often about the school in Paris we had both attended. We became girlfriend and boyfriend during our second year at Lycée Henri-IV. And we fell in love exactly the way teenagers do—with unstoppable passion. There wasn't enough time in the day for all the laughter and talking and sex that we needed to have. Even when we broke up, just before we both left for university, we did it with excessive passion. Lots of door slamming and yelling and crying and kissing.

Ten years later, when Act II of *The Story of Dalia and Luc* began, it was as if we were teenagers all over again. First of all, we "met cute." Dalia and I reconnected completely accidentally three months ago at one of the rare NYPD social functions—a spring boat ride on the Hudson River. I was standing alone at the starboard railing and must have been turning green. About to heave, I was one seasick sailor.

"You look like a man who needs some Dramamine," came Dalia's voice from behind me. I'd know it anywhere. I turned around.

"Holy shit! It's you," I said. We hugged and immediately agreed that only God himself could have planned this meeting. It may not have been an actual miracle, but it was certainly *une coïncidence grande*. Two former Parisian lovers who end up on a boat and then…

Dalia reminded me that she was not Parisian. She was Israeli, a sabra.

"Okay, then it's a fairy tale," I said. "And in fairy tales you don't pay attention to details."

By the time the boat docked at Chelsea Piers, we were in love again. And—holy shit indeed—had she ever turned from a spectacular-looking teenager into an incredibly spectacular-looking young woman.

She invited me back to her ridiculously large penthouse at 15 Central Park West, the apartment that her father, the film director and producer Menashe Boaz, had paid for. That night was beyond unforgettable. I couldn't imagine my life if that night had never happened.

After the first week, I had most of my clothes sent over.

After the second week, I had my exercise bike and weights sent over.

After a month I hired a company to deliver the three most valuable pieces from my contemporary Chinese art collection: the Zao Wou-Ki, the Zhang Xiaogang, and the Zeng Fanzhi. Dalia refers to them as the Z-name contemporary art collection. She said that when those paintings were hung in her living room, she knew I planned to stay.

But now we have *this* night. The night of Maria's death. A night that's the emotional opposite of that joyful night months ago.

"Will you be hungry later on?" Dalia asks.

"I doubt it," I say. I pour us each another glass of wine. "Anyway, if we get hungry later on, I'll make us some scrambled eggs."

She smiles and says, "An eight-burner Garland range and we're making scrambled eggs."

That statement should be cute and funny. But we both know that nothing can be cute and funny this evening.

"I want to ask you something," I say.

"Yeah, of course," she says. She wrinkles her forehead a tiny bit. As if she's expecting some scary question. I proceed.

"Are you angry that I'm so sad about Maria's murder?"

Dalia pauses. Then she tilts her head to the side. Her face is now soft, tender, caring.

"Oh, Luc," she says. "I would only be angry if you were *not* sad."

I feel that we should kiss. I think Dalia feels the same way. But I also think something inside each of us is telling us that if we did kiss, no matter how chaste the kiss might be, it would be almost disrespectful to Maria.

We sit silently for a long time. We finish the bottle of Chardonnay.

It turns out that we never were hungry enough to scramble some eggs. All we did was wait for the day to end.

CHAPTER 10

THE PERSON RESPONSIBLE FOR whatever skill I have in speaking decent English—very little French accent, pretty good English vocabulary—is Inspector Nick Elliott. No one has mastered the art of plain speaking better than he has.

"Morning, Pretty Boy. Looks like it's going to be a shitty day" is a typical example.

This morning Elliott and a woman I've never seen before appear at my desk. Looks like I'm about to receive an extra lesson in basic communication skills.

"Moncrief, meet Katherine Burke. You two are going to be partners in the Martinez investigation. I don't care to discuss it."

I barely have time to register the woman's face when he adds, "Good luck. Now get the hell to work."

"But sir…" I begin.

"Is there a problem?" Elliott asks, clearly anxious to hit the road.

"Well, no, but…"

"Good. Here's the deal. Katherine Burke is a detective, a *New York* detective, and has been for almost two years. She knows police procedure better than most people know their own names. She can teach you a lot."

I go for the end-run charm play.

"And I've got a lot to learn," I say, a big smile on my face.

He doesn't smile back.

"Don't get me wrong," Elliott says as he turns and speaks to Burke. "Moncrief has the instincts of a good detective. He just needs a little spit and polish."

As he walks away, I look at Katherine Burke. She is not Maria Martinez. So, of course, I immediately hate her.

"Good to meet you," she says.

"Same here." We shake, more like a quick touch of the hands.

My new partner and I study each other quietly, closely. We are like a bride and groom in a prearranged marriage meeting for the first time. This "marriage" means a great deal to me—joy, sorrow, and whether or not I can smoke in the squad car.

So what do I see before me? Burke is thirty-two, I'd guess. Face: pretty. No, actually *très jolie*. Irish; pale; big red lips. A good-looking woman in too-tight khakis. She seems pleasant enough. But I'm not sensing "warm and friendly."

And what does she see? A guy with an expensive haircut, an expensive suit, and—I think she's figured out already—a pretty bad attitude.

This does not bode well.

"Listen," she says. "I know this is tough for you. The inspector told me how much you admired Maria. We can talk about that."

"No," I say. "We can forget about that."

Silence again. Then I speak.

"Look. I apologize. You were trying to be nice, and I was just being…well…"

She fills it in for me: "A rude asshole. It happens to the best of us."

I smile, and I move a step closer. I read the official ID card that hangs from the cord around her neck. It shows her NYPD number and, in the same size type, her title. These are followed by her name in big bold uppercase lettering:

K. BURKE

"So you want to be called K. Burke?" I ask her as we walk back to the detective room.

"No. Katherine, Katie, or Kathy. Any of those are fine," she says.

"Then why do you have 'K. Burke' printed on your ID?"

"That's what they put there when they gave me the ID," she says. "The ID badge wasn't high on my priority list."

"K. Burke. I like it. From now on, that's what I'm going to call you. K. Burke."

She nods. For a few moments we don't speak. Then I say, "But I must be honest with you, K. Burke. I don't think this is going to work out."

She speaks, still seriously.

"You want to know something, Detective Moncrief?"

"What?"

"I think you're right."

And then, for the first time, she smiles.

CHAPTER 11

THE LOBBY OF THE Auberge du Parc Hotel is somebody's idea of elegance. But it sure as hell is not mine.

"Pink marble on the walls *and* the floor *and* the ceiling. If Barbie owned a brothel it would look like this." I share this observation with my new partner as I look out the floor-to-ceiling windows that face Park Avenue.

K. Burke either doesn't get the joke or doesn't like the joke. No laughter.

"We're not here to evaluate the decor," she says. "You know better than I do that Auberge du Parc is right up there with the Plaza and the Carlyle when it comes to expensive hotels for rich people."

"And it affords a magnificent view of the building where Maria Martinez was killed," I say as I gesture to the tall windows.

Burke looks out to the corner of 68th Street and Park Avenue. She nods solemnly. "That's why we're starting the job here."

"The job, you will agree, is fairly stupid?" I ask.

"The job is what Inspector Elliott has assigned us, and I'm not about to second-guess the command," she says.

Elliott wants us to interview prostitutes, streetwalkers, anyone he defines as "high-class lowlife." Enormously upscale hotels like the Auberge often have a lot of illegal sex stuff going on behind their pink marble walls. But asking the devils to tell us their sins? I don't think so.

This approach is ridiculous, to my way of thinking. Solutions come mostly by listening for small surprises—and yes, sometimes by looking for a few intelligent pieces of hard evidence. Looking in the *unlikely* places. Talking to the *least* likely observers.

Burke's theory, which is total NYPD style, is way more traditional: "You accumulate the information," she had said. "You assemble the puzzle piece by piece."

"Absolutely not," I replied. "You sink into the case as if it were a warm bath. You *sense* the situation. You look for the fingerprint of the crime itself." Then I added, "Here's what we'll do: you'll do it your way. I'll do it mine."

"No, not *your* way or *my* way," she had said. "We'll do it the NYPD way."

That discussion was a half hour ago. Now I'm really too disgusted and frustrated to say anything else.

So I stand with my new partner in a pink marble lobby a few hundred yards from where my old partner was murdered.

Okay. I'll be the adult here. I will try to appear cooperative.

We review our plan. I am to go to the lobby bar and talk to the one or two high-priced hookers who are almost always on the prowl there. You've seen them—the girls with the perfect hair falling gently over their shoulders. The delicate pointy noses all supplied by the same plastic surgeon. The women who are drinking in the afternoon while they're dressed for the evening.

Burke will go up to the more elegant, more secluded rooftop bar, Auberge in the Clouds. But of course she'll first stop by the hotel manager's office and tell him what he already knows: the NYPD is here. Procedure, procedure, procedure.

If Maria Martinez is watching all this from some heavenly locale, she is falling on the floor laughing.

After agreeing to meet Burke back in the lobby in forty-five minutes, I walk into the bar. (I once visited Versailles on a high school class trip, and this place would have pleased Marie Antoinette.) The bar itself is a square-shaped ebony box with gold curlicues all over it. It looks like a huge birthday present for a god with no taste.

At the bar sit two pretty ladies, one in a red silk dress, the other in a kind of clingy Diane von Furstenberg green-and-white thing, which is very loose around the top. I don't think von Furstenberg designed it to be so erotic. It takes me about two seconds to realize what these women do for a living.

These girls are precisely the type that Nick Elliott wants us to speak to. Yes, a ridiculous waste of time. And I know just what to do about it.

I walk toward the exit and push through the revolving door.

I'm out. I'm on my own. This is more like it.

CHAPTER 12

K. BURKE THINKS A good New York cop solves a case by putting the pieces together. K. Burke is wrong.

You can't put the pieces together in New York because there are just too goddamn many of them.

One step out the revolving door onto East 68th Street proves my point. It's only midday, but everywhere I look there's chaos and color and confusion.

Bike messengers and homeless people and dowagers and grammar-school students. Two women wheeling a full-size gold harp and two guys pushing a wheelbarrow full of bricks. The Greenpeace recruiter with her clipboard and smile, the crazy half-naked lady waving a broken umbrella, and the teenager selling iPad cases. All this on one block.

The store next to the Auberge bar entrance is called Spa-Roe. According to the sign, it's a place you can visit for facials and massages (the "spa" part) while you sample various caviars (the "roe" part). Just what the world has been waiting for.

Right next to it is a bistro…*pardon*…a bar. It's called Fitzgerald's, as in "F. Scott." I stand in front of it for a few moments and look through the window. It's a re-creation of a 1920s speakeasy. I can see a huge poster that says GOD BLESS JIMMY WALKER. Only one person is seated at the bar, a pretty young blond girl. She's chatting with the much older bartender.

I walk about twenty feet and pass a pet-grooming store. A very unhappy cat is being shampooed. Next door is a "French" dry cleaner, a term I'd never heard before moving to New York. There's an optician who sells *discounted* Tom Ford eyeglass frames for four hundred dollars. There's a place to have your computer fixed and a place that sells nothing but brass buttons. I pause. I smoke a cigarette. The block is busy as hell, but nothing is happening for me.

Until I toss my cigarette on the sidewalk.

CHAPTER 13

A MAN'S VOICE ISN'T ANGRY, just loud. "What's with the littering, mister?"

Littering? That's a new word in my English vocabulary.

The speaker is a white-bearded old man wearing brown work pants and a brown T-shirt. It's the kind of outfit assembled to look like a uniform, but it isn't actually a uniform. The man is barely five feet tall. He holds an industrial-size water hose with a dripping nozzle.

"Littering?" I ask.

The old guy points to the dead cigarette at my feet.

"Your cigarette! They pay me to keep these sidewalks clean."

"I apologize."

"I was making a joke. It's only a joke. Get it? A joke, just a joke."

This man was not completely, uh...mentally competent, but I had to follow one of my major rules: talk to anyone, anywhere, anytime.

"Yes, a joke. Good. Do you live here?" I ask.

"The Bronx," he answers. "Mott Haven. They always call it the south Bronx, but it's not. I don't know why they can't get it right."

"So you just work down here?"

"Yeah. I watch the three buildings. The button place, the animal place, and the eyeglasses place. They call me Danny with the Hose."

"Understandably," I say.

"Good, you understand. Now stand back."

I do as I'm told until my back is up against the optician's doorway. Danny sprays the sidewalk with a fast hard surge of water. Scraps of paper, chunks of dog shit, empty beer cans—they all go flying into the gutter.

"Danny," I say. "A lot of pretty girls around here, huh? What with the fancy hotel right here and the fancy neighborhood."

He shuts off his hose. "Some are pretty. I mind my business."

A young man, no more than twenty-five, comes out of the pet-grooming shop. He has a big dog—a boxer, I think—on a leash. Danny with the Hose and the man with the dog greet each other with a high five. The young man is tall, blond, good-looking. He wears long blue shorts and a pathetic red sleeveless shirt.

"Hey," I say to him. "Danny and I have just been talking about the neighborhood. I'm moving to East 68th Street in a few weeks. With a roommate. A German shepherd."

"Cool," he says, suddenly a lot more interested in talking to me. "If you need a groomer, this place is the best. Take a look at Titan." He pets his dog's shiny coat. "He's handsome enough to be in a *GQ* spread. I've been bringing him here ever since we moved into 655 Park five years ago."

My ears prick up. I go into full acting-class mode now.

"Isn't 655 the place where that lady cop got killed?"

"They say she was a cop pretending to be a hooker. I don't know."

"Luc…Luc Moncrief," I say. We shake.

"Eric," he says. No last name offered. "Well, welcome. I said 'pretending,' but I don't know. Women are not my area of expertise, if you know what I mean. All my info on the local girls comes from one of the doormen in my building. He says all the hookers hang out at the Auberge."

"That's where I'm staying now," I say.

"Well, anyway, Carl—the doorman—says most of the girls who work out of the Auberge bar are clean. Bang, bang, pay your money, over and out. He says the ones to watch out for are the girls who work for the Russians. Younger and prettier, but they'll skin you alive. I dunno. I play on a whole other team."

"Yet you seem to know a great deal about *mine*," I say. "Nice meeting you."

The guy and the dog take off. Danny with the Hose has disappeared, too.

I look at my watch. I should be meeting up with K. Burke.

But first I'll just go on a quick errand.

CHAPTER 14

IF YOU EVER NEED to get some information from a New York doorman, learn from my experience with Carl.

A ten-dollar bill will get you this: "Yeah, I think there's some foreign kind of operation going on at the Auberge. But I'm busy getting taxis for people and helping with packages. So I can't be sure."

I give Carl another ten dollars.

"They got Russians in and outta there. At least I think they're Russian. I'm not that good with accents."

I give him ten more. That's thirty so far, if you're keeping track.

"I heard all this from a friend who works catering at the Auberge. The Russians keep a permanent three-room suite there… where they pimp out the hookers."

Carl gives me a sly smile. It would seem my reaction has given away my motives.

"Oh, I see where you're headed. You wanna know if the Russians had anything to do with the murder on seven. The cops talked to me, like, twenty times. But I wasn't on the door that day. And how the girl got in? No clue."

Perhaps that's true. But I have a feeling Carl might be leading me to some other clues. I give him ten bucks more.

"Strange, though. Those Russians specialize in young, pretty, all-American blondes. You know. Fresh, clean, sort of look like innocent little virgins. Nothing like the woman who got iced. But…there is something else."

I wait for Carl to keep talking, but he doesn't. Instead, he hustles outside the building just as a yellow cab pulls up. He opens the door, and a weary-looking gray-haired man in a gray pin-striped suit emerges. Carl takes the man's briefcase and follows him down a long hallway that leads to an elevator. The old man might as well be *crawling*, he's going so slowly. Finally Carl returns.

"Sorry. Now, what was I saying?"

Damn this sneaky doorman. I know he's playing me, but I'm hoping it's worth it. Because all I've got left is a fifty. I give it to Carl with a soft warning: "This better be worth fifty bucks."

"Well, it's a little thing, and it's from my buddy at the Auberge, and you never know when he's telling the truth, and…"

"Come on. What is it?"

"He says that the girls never wait in the lobby or the suite or the back hallways. The Russian guys keep 'em in the neighborhood somewhere. I don't know where. Like a coffee shop or a private house. Then the girl gets a phone call and a few minutes later one of the blondies is taking the elevator up to the special private suite."

Bingo. I'm ready to roll. And—if you're keeping track—it cost me ninety bucks.

But it was *definitely* worth it.

CHAPTER 15

I WALK INTO THE lobby of the Auberge. Standing there is K. Burke. She's easily identifiable by the smoke coming out of her ears.

"Where have you been?" she demands. "I checked the bar, then the restaurants, then…anyway. What did you find out?"

"Nothing," I say. "And you?"

"Wait a minute. Nothing? How many people did you talk to?"

"*Beaucoup.*"

"And nothing?"

"*Oui. Rien.*"

She shakes her head, but I'm not sure she believes me.

"Well," she says as she gestures me out the front door, "while I was standing around, waiting for a certain someone I won't name, I texted a contact in Vice, who gave me access to some of their files. And I have a theory." Detective Burke begins to speak more quickly now, but she still sounds like a first-grade teacher explaining simple arithmetic to the class.

"There have been three call-girl murders in the past three months, including Maria Martinez. All Vice cops posing as call girls. The first was…"

I cannot keep quiet. We've already looked into this.

"I know," I say. "Valerie Delvecchio. Murdered at a construction site. A *rénovation* of a hotel. The Hotel Chelsea, on 23rd Street and Seventh Avenue. The second cop was Dana Morgan-Schwarz. She was offed in a hotel on 155th and Riverside. A drug-den SRO so bad I wouldn't go there to take a piss."

This does nothing to dampen Burke's enthusiasm for her theory.

"Don't you see, Moncrief? You're not putting the pieces together. This is a pattern. Three Vice cops posing as call girls. All of them murdered. This is—"

"This is ridiculous," I say. "This is *not* a *pattern*. It is at best a *coincidence*. The Chelsea murder is unsolved, yes. But the detective's body was dumped there *after* she was murdered. And Morgan-Schwarz was probably involved in an inside drug deal. No high-class hooker would go to that hotel."

But Burke is simply not listening.

"I set up a meeting for us with Vice this afternoon at four. We're going to get the names, numbers, and websites of *every* expensive call-girl service in New York."

"Good luck with that," I say. "That should only take a few weeks."

"Then we're going to meet all the people who run them. I don't care if it's the Mafia, Brazilian drug lords, Colombian cartels, or other cops. We're going to see every last one."

"Great. That should only take a few *months*."

"You've got a bad goddamn attitude, Moncrief."

I'm not going to explode. I'm not going to explode. I'm not going to explode.

"I will see you at four o'clock for our meeting with Vice," I say calmly.

"Where are you going till then? We've got work to do."

"I'm going to work right now. Want to come along?"

Burke folds her arms and frowns. "You lied to me, didn't you? You did find out something."

"Come with me and see for yourself."

CHAPTER 16

"**WELCOME TO THE ROARING** Twenties," I say to K. Burke as we enter Fitzgerald's Bar and Grill, on East 68th Street.

"Not much roaring going on," Burke says. The room is empty except for the bartender and one female customer.

The same girl I watched through the window earlier.

The lone woman at the bar is young. She's blond. She's pretty. And after we flash IDs and introduce ourselves as detectives with the NYPD, she's also very frightened.

"Try to relax, miss," says Burke. "There's a problem, but it's nothing for you to worry about. We're just hoping you can help us out."

I'm astonished at the genuine sweetness in Detective Burke's voice. The same voice that was just loud and stern with me is now soothing and gentle with the pretty blonde.

"Could you tell us your name, please?" I ask, trying to imitate Burke's soft style.

"Laura," she says. Her voice has a quiver of fear.

"What about a last name?" Burke asks.

"Jenkins," says the girl. "Laura Jenkins."

"Let's see some ID," I say.

The girl rustles around in her pocketbook and produces a laminated card. Burke doesn't even look at it.

"You're aware, Ms. Jenkins, that in the state of New York, showing a police officer false identification is a class D felony punishable by up to seven years in prison."

Holy shit. I'm in awe of Burke. Sort of.

The girl slips the first card she removed from her purse back into it and hands over a second. It reads: LAURA DELARICO, 21 ARDSLEY ROAD, SCARSDALE, NEW YORK.

"What do you do for a living, Miss Delarico?" I ask.

"I'm a law student. That's the truth. I go to Fordham. Here's my student ID." She holds up a third plastic identity card.

"Do you work?" I ask. "Perhaps part-time?"

"Sometimes I babysit. I do computer filing for one of the professors."

"Look, Miss Delarico," I say, raising my voice now. "This is serious business. Very serious. Detective Burke was being genuine when she said you have nothing to worry about. But that only happens if you help us out. So far, not good. Not good at all."

Laura looks away, then back at me.

"We know that you work for a prostitution ring," I continue. "A group that trades in high-priced call girls. We know it's controlled by a Russian gang."

Laura begins to cry. "But I'm a law student. Really."

"A few days ago a female detective posing as a call girl was murdered. Somebody who meant a lot to me. We need your help."

I pause. Not for dramatic effect but because I feel myself choking up, too.

Laura stops crying long enough to say, "It's just something I'm doing for a little while. For the money. I live with my grandfather, and law school costs so much. If he ever found out…"

A few seconds pass.

Then K. Burke says, "Off the record."

K. Burke is staring deep into Laura's eyes. But Laura is frozen. No response.

"Let me show you something," I say.

Laura looks suspicious. K. Burke looks confused. I reach into my side pocket. Next to my ID, next to the place where I kept the cash for Carl the doorman, are two small photographs. I take them out. One shows Maria Martinez on the police department's Hudson River boat ride. I took that picture. The other shows Maria Martinez dead. It was taken by the coroner.

I show Laura the photos. Then she looks away.

Finally, she says, "Okay."

CHAPTER 17

PROSTITUTES DON'T KEEP traditional hours.

Laura Delarico tells us that she's "on call" at Fitzgerald's for another thirty minutes. She's certain she'll be free by late afternoon. "Even if I do get a client," she says, "I'll be in and out quickly." (No, I don't think she was trying to be funny.)

I suggest that Laura, K. Burke, and I meet at Balthazar, where a person can get a decent *steak frites* and a pleasant glass of house Burgundy. "This will put everyone at ease," I say.

K. Burke suggests that we schedule an interview at the precinct this evening. "This is an investigation, Moncrief, not happy hour. Plus, *I'm* going to that meeting with Vice."

Because proper police procedure always trumps a good idea, at six o'clock the three of us are sitting in an interrogation room at the precinct.

Laura is surprisingly interested in the surroundings. The bile-colored green walls, the battered folding chairs, the crushed empty cans of Diet Coke on the table. I don't think I'm wrong in thinking that Laura is also interested in me.

"So this is, like, where you bring murderers, drug dealers, and…okay, prostitutes?"

"Sometimes," I say. "But today is strictly informal, off the record. No recordings, no cameras, but as much of the cold tan sludge my colleagues call coffee as you can drink."

Laura is wearing a black T-shirt, jeans, and a gold necklace with the name *Laura* on it. She could be a barista at Starbucks or a salesgirl at the Gap or, yes, a law student.

"We're very glad that you agreed to try to help us," K. Burke begins.

Laura interrupts: "Listen. I don't think I want to do this anymore. I think I've changed my mind."

"That would not be a good idea," I say. My goal is not to sound threatening, merely disappointed.

"We're counting on you," K. Burke says. Where does she hide that beautiful soothing voice?

"I don't think there's much I *can* tell you," Laura says. "I get a call. I turn a trick. That's how it goes."

"Tell us anything," I say.

"Anything?" Laura says. Her voice is suddenly loud, suddenly scared. "Like what? What does 'anything' mean? What I ate for lunch? What classes I went to? Anything?"

The conversation needs K. Burke's smooth-as-silk voice. Here it comes.

"Maria Martinez was found murdered on Tuesday," K. Burke says. "Were you working Tuesday morning or Monday night?"

Laura closes her eyes. Her lips curl with disgust. She spits out three little words: "Paulo the Pig."

Burke and I are, of course, confused. I picture a cartoon character in a Spanish children's television program.

But Laura repeats it, this time with even more venom. "Paulo the Pig."

"That's a person, I assume," Burke says.

"A person who deserves his nickname. If you're a girl on call and you get assigned to Paulo the Pig, you never forget it."

Her hands shake a bit. Her eyes begin to water.

"That's where I was the night your friend was murdered. I was with Paulo. Paulo Montes."

"Tell us, Laura," I say. "We need to know what happened that night with you and Paulo. Everything you remember. You're safe with us."

Her story is disgusting.

CHAPTER 18

Auberge du Parc Hotel
Monday evening

PAULO MONTES, A BRAZILIAN drug dealer, is usually followed everywhere by two bodyguards. Tonight, however, he sends them away and waits alone for the arrival of his hired girl.

The fat middle-aged man has dressed appropriately for the occasion—a sweat-soaked sleeveless undershirt. Thick curly black hair grows like an unmown lawn over both Paulo's chest and back. The hairs crawl up and down his shoulders and neck. He wears long white silk shorts—longer than boxers, almost long enough to touch his fleshy pink knees. Montes has greased himself up with a nauseating combination of almond oil and lavender cologne. He has used this same overwhelming oil-and-cologne concoction to slick back the greasy hair above his fat round face.

Paulo answers the door himself. "You're much prettier than that dark-haired bitch they sent up an hour ago," he says.

He is speaking to Laura Delarico—tall, slim, blond. With her fine youthful features, Laura is easily Paulo's fantasy come to life— a combination of Texas cheerleader and Italian fashion model. Fresh and clean, lithe and athletic. Just what Paulo is longing for.

He begins quickly, clumsily unbuttoning Laura's white oxford-cloth shirt. "The first one they sent was the kind I could find for ten dollars in an alley in São Paulo. Dark hair, dark skin. Screwing her would be like screwing myself."

Paulo Montes laughs uproariously at his little joke. Laura smiles. She's been taught to smile at a client's jokes.

Paulo pulls her onto the bed. His fingers are fat, and he has become bored with trying to unbutton Laura's shirt. So he pulls it up and over her head. He tugs at Laura's panties, ripping them.

Soon she is naked. Soon Paulo the Pig is naked. Every inch of Laura's flesh is disgusted by him. She feels he might crush her with his weight, but she's skilled at positioning her shoulders and hips in such a way as to minimize all discomfort. She tries to ignore the garlicky alcohol smell as he roughly kisses her face and lips, as he squirms slowly downward to kiss her breasts. He suddenly slaps her face. For some sick reason this makes him laugh. Paulo Montes then pulls hard at her hair.

"Stop it," Laura says. "You're hurting me."

"Like I give a shit," Paulo says. Now he grabs her genitals. His filthy fingernails travel harshly around her vagina. She feels scratching, bleeding. With his other hand he pulls hard at another handful of hair. "I'm paying good money for this!" he yells. "I'm in charge."

He pushes himself back up, again closer to her face. His saliva is dripping onto Laura's cheeks and lips. The kisses begin to feel more like bites. She is certain the skin on her right cheek has been punctured by his teeth. Then more hair pulling. Her vagina is full of pain.

This time Laura screams. "Stop. Slow down!" She pushes at his fat neck.

Then suddenly Paulo makes a huge noise—a kind of explosive grunt. His breathing immediately slows down.

Laura realizes that she doesn't need to protest any longer. It's over. He's finished. He never even entered her. Paulo the Pig begins panting like a tired old horse. He is resting, she thinks. He remains on top of her for a few minutes.

Finally Paulo rolls off and rests at her side.

For a moment, Laura becomes a kind of waitress in a sexual diner. "Can I get you anything else, sir?"

But Paulo Montes merely keeps his heavy breathing pumping. "That was good, very good. Go into the next room. Take what you want. Within reason, of course." He laughs again. What a comedian!

Like all the girls who work for the Russian gang, Laura knows Paulo Montes is one of the most significant importers of what are called travel packages: drugs that are smuggled along strange geographic routes—say, from Ankara to Kiev to Seoul to New York to São Paulo—in order to confuse and evade the narcs.

"No, thank you," Laura says, slipping into her torn underwear, her jeans, and her shirt. She plucks a few of his many sweaty curly hairs from her stomach.

"Don't be ungrateful, bitch," Paulo says. This time he's not sounding funny. He doesn't laugh. "Scag, maybe. I got it in the plastic containers. Or some good China white."

"I just need to use the bathroom," Laura says.

Paulo snaps at her quickly. "Use the maid's bathroom at the end of the hall. You can't use this one. I have personal items in there."

Laura simply says, "Okay." She's tired and frightened and disgusted.

"Now go in the next room and treat yourself. Even something simple. Take a little C. Have a party later with your friends."

To appease him she says, "Do you have some weed? I'll take some weed."

He laughs again, the loudest of all his laughing jags.

"Weed? You're joking. Like Paulo would ever deal low-class shit like that."

She watches Paulo on the bed, naked, laughing.

As Laura leaves the room all she can think of is that line from the Christmas poem: "…a little round belly / That shook when he laughed, like a bowl full of jelly."

CHAPTER 19

LAURA DELARICO HAS FINISHED her story.

"So that's it. The clients don't pay us girls directly. It's all online, I guess. I don't really know. When it was over, I just left."

Burke speaks. "Detective Moncrief and I want to thank you. We know this has been tough."

"I wish I could have helped more," Laura says. "I'm not afraid. I just…well, that's what happened."

"You've helped us more than you can imagine," I say. Sincerely, softly. "What you gave us was big. I'm fairly certain Maria Martinez visited Paulo's room as well."

Burke agrees. "There's a very real possibility she was the dark-haired girl he rejected before you."

"You don't know that for sure," Laura says.

"You're right," I say. "Not yet. But it is a logical deduction. He may have killed her and disposed of her. *Or* he may have put her body in the bathroom."

"The one he wouldn't let me use," she says quietly. "I guess that makes sense."

K. Burke holds up her hand. "Or we may be completely off base. Maybe it was not Maria Martinez. Maybe we've got it all wrong."

I cannot resist. I say, "Ah, K. Burke, ever the jolly optimist."

I reach over and gently touch Laura Delarico's hand. She does not pull away. She is so much less frightened than she was a few hours ago.

"And that is why…" Suddenly, I must stop speaking. Oh, shit. Oh, no.

I feel my throat begin to burn. I'm having trouble breathing. Maria is on my mind, in my heart. Because of Laura's information, we may actually have a shot at solving Maria's murder.

K. Burke senses the emotional hole I've fallen into. She finishes my remarks.

"And that's why…we need you to help us just a little bit more."

CHAPTER 20

LAURA SAYS NOTHING FOR a few long moments.

"Well?" I say.

Laura is suddenly businesslike. Sharp. Composed.

"I know what you'll do if I don't keep helping you," she says.

"You *know* what we'll do?" I ask. "I don't even know what we'll do except ask you to help us."

"No," Laura says. "You'll play the Grandpa card."

"The what?" I ask.

K. Burke is far quicker than I am in this matter.

"Laura thinks we'll tell her grandfather how she's been making money," says Burke.

For the first time I see a toughness in Laura. I am beginning to think that Laura Delarico is not so naive and innocent as I first thought. She'll make a good lawyer someday.

"Believe whatever you want, Laura," I say, "but I promise you with my heart that we will never do such a thing."

"I guess I'll believe you because…well, because I *want* to believe you," Laura says. "I want to help…at least, I think I want to help. Oh, this sucks. This whole thing sucks."

Time for a bottom line. Laura agrees to continue to help. "But just one more time."

Later, after Laura leaves, K. Burke and I walk the dirty gray hallway back to the detective room.

"Nice job," Burke says. "Your performance won her over."

"Did you think that was a performance, K. Burke?" I ask.

"To be honest, I don't know."

Back at our desks, we learn that Paulo Montes will not be in New York for three days. He is on a quick drug trip through San Juan, Havana, and Kingston.

I tell Burke that I'm going to take one of those three days off.

"Impossible!" she exclaims. "Your presence is critical. We have Vice files to examine. We have a reinspection of the murder scene as well as forensics at Montes's suite. I need you to—"

I cut her off immediately. "Hold it," I say sharply. "Here's what I need from *you*. I need you to stop thinking that you're my boss. You're my partner. And I don't mean to throw this in your face, K. Burke, but we would not be progressing if I had not pursued my very *un*professional way of doing things."

K. Burke gives me her version of a sincere smile. Then she says, "Whatever you say, partner."

CHAPTER 21

A MAN KNOWS HE'S in love when he's totally happy just watching his girlfriend do even the simplest things—peeling an apple, combing her hair, fluffing up a bed pillow, laughing.

That is precisely how I'm feeling when I walk into the ridiculously tricked-out media room of Dalia's apartment: the Apologue speakers, the Supernova One screen, the leather Eames chairs. A room that is insanely lavish and almost never used.

As I walk in I see Dalia standing on a stepladder. Her back is to me. She is frantically sorting through the small closet high above the wet bar. She neither sees nor hears me enter. I stand and watch her for a moment. I smile. Dalia is wearing jeans and a turquoise T-shirt. As she stretches, one or two inches of her lower back are exposed.

I walk toward her and kiss her gently on that enticing lower back.

She gives a quick little yell.

"Don't be scared," I say. "It's only me."

She steps off the ladder and we embrace fully. I know a great kiss cannot wash away a bad day, but it surely can make the night seem a little bit brighter.

"When did *this* closet become the junk closet?" she asks as she climbs back up the ladder and begins tossing things down to me.

A plastic bag of poker chips. These are followed by three Scrabble tiles (*W, E,* and the always important *X*). A plastic box containing ivory chess pieces, but no chessboard in sight. And a true relic from the Victorian era: a Game Boy.

"This is for you," she says as she pretends to hit me on the head with a wooden croquet mallet. I add the mallet to the ever-expanding pile of items next to me.

"And you'll like *this,*" she says with a smile. Dalia leans down and hands me a small gold box. I open it. It contains two little bronze balls the size of small marbles. Never saw them before. I shrug.

"Give up?" she asks. "They're those Chinese things they use for sex, for the vagina."

"The vagina?" I say. "Yes. I think I've heard of it." She laughs and punches me lightly on the arm. I decide not to ask where she got them—or how often she used them or with whom.

"Well," she says. "At least we've solved *one* mystery. This closet is not a junk closet. It is obviously a game closet."

"What exactly are you looking for, anyway?" I ask.

"This," she says as she steps down off the ladder. She is holding a slim burgundy leather book. I recognize it immediately. It's the yearbook for our class at Lycée Henri-IV.

She opens it and turns to the page that has her graduation picture. "I was thinking of getting bangs. The last time I had them was when I was a kid. I wanted to see if I was as goofy-looking as I remember." She frowns. "Guess I was."

I say exactly what is expected of a man in this situation. The only difference is that this man means it with all his heart.

"You were beautiful," I say.

"You're mad. Braids on the side and bangs in the front. I look like a goatherd."

I reach toward her and touch her face.

"If so, then you are *la plus belle* goatherd since the beginning of time." I lean in and kiss her. Then I speak. "How about we have something nice to drink?"

"How about a nice warm bath, with lavender perfume?" she says.

"A bath?" I say. "I don't know. I don't think I'm *that* thirsty."

Dalia taps me playfully on my nose. Then she heads toward the bathroom.

CHAPTER 22

Auberge du Parc Hotel
Three days later
1:20 a.m.

LAURA KNOCKS ON THE hotel-room door. Everything feels just as it did the last time she visited Paulo.

She wears a white oxford-cloth shirt. Just as she did the last time. The tiny entrance hall where she waits stinks of liquor and bad cologne. Just as it did the last time. One other thing that's the same, one other thing she cannot deny: she's horribly frightened. Her arm shakes as she knocks on the door again.

Yes, Moncrief and Burke have assured her that everything is set up to keep her perfectly safe. This time, hidden in Paulo's bedroom are two minuscule video surveillance cameras: one is attached to a large bronze lamp on the writing desk, the other to the fake gold-leaf-and-crystal chandelier hanging directly over the king-size bed. The videos play on monitors that are being watched two doors away by five people: Luc Moncrief, K. Burke, Inspector Nick Elliott, and two officers from Vice.

Paulo opens the door and steps back. He smiles at her.

This time Paulo manages to look even more disgusting than

before. Laura Delarico quietly gasps as she takes in the repellent sight: Paulo the Pig is completely naked except for a pair of short brown socks.

"So," he says. "They sent you back like I asked. I'm glad. You're the best."

Laura and the five people watching in the other room realize immediately that Paulo Montes is drunk or drugged or both. He stumbles. He slurs his words. His feeble erection collapses as he lunges toward her, and he begins half spitting and half kissing, half hugging and half groping her.

"Hold on. Come on. Just hold on," Laura says. Then she uses one of the first conversation starters that a woman learns in "prostitute school."

"Let's get to know each other."

Laura wonders how she will ever get Paulo to talk about the dark-haired woman, the woman who may have been Maria Martinez. Laura wafts in and out of that nightmare. She must keep reminding herself she is there to help uncover the truth of the death of a woman she never even knew.

Paulo is even more impatient this time at bat. He tugs hard at Laura's shirt. Two buttons snap off and onto the floor. He pushes his greasy face into her breasts as if he is trying to suck in oxygen from the space between them.

Within a few seconds, he has her on the bed. They are, for the moment, side by side, facing each other. The slobbering. The saliva. The boozy breath.

"So," Laura ventures, trying to cajole him into a calmer, gentler mood. "Just tell me how much more you like me than that dark-haired girl who was here."

Paulo is in no mood for conversation. He is somewhere between crazy drunk and crazy turned on.

"Dark?" he shouts. "Was her hair dark? I don't remember. Does any bitch have the color she's born with? In Brazil they all lie. Lie and dye. That's the joke in Rio and São Paulo. Let's check you. Let's see if you're telling the truth."

Laura fears a harsh inspection of her pubic hair. Instead Montes rolls over and on top of her. He grabs a great chunk of her hair and pulls it hard with his fat heavy hands. She yells for him to stop.

"I have to find the roots!" he screams and laughs simultaneously.

In the surveillance room, Inspector Elliott speaks loudly: "We've got to stop this immediately, Moncrief. We can haul him in right now for aggravated assault."

"I don't want him arrested. I want him to talk," says Moncrief. "I want to get the story on Maria."

"I swear, Moncrief. This whole thing is a half-assed setup. I should never have let it get this far."

"Inspector! Look!" K. Burke says. All five in the surveillance group peer intently at the screen. Paulo Montes is grunting and making animal-like noises as he pinches one of Laura's nipples hard and fiercely bites the other.

"That's it!" yells Elliott.

"Give it five seconds," says Moncrief as he grabs Elliott by the arm to urge him to remain. "The guy might calm down."

Almost as if Montes actually heard Moncrief speak, Paulo begins gently massaging Laura's breasts.

"There, there," Paulo says softly. "You are beautiful. I could love a woman like you."

Paulo gently brushes his lips against Laura's beautiful soft cheeks. He touches her chin and runs his hand down her neck.

"Kiss me," Paulo says. "Kiss me like you love me."

Laura knows her job. She kisses him softly on his lips.

Then suddenly, horribly, Montes slaps Laura violently against her right cheek, so violently that her head snaps to the side. She lets out a scream.

"You are just another dumb bitch," Montes shouts, saliva dripping from his mouth onto Laura's face.

"Get away!" Laura screams. "Get the hell off of me!"

Paulo slaps her again, then holds her down by her wrists. She is fighting as hard as she can. But it's useless.

Again she screams, "Get off! Stop it!"

As Paulo is about to sink his teeth into her, the door to the room swings open.

"NYPD! Freeze!" The voice belongs to Moncrief.

Moncrief, Burke, and both Vice officers are holding guns. They all rush toward the bed.

With the help of one of the Vice cops, Moncrief pulls Montes away from Laura.

Laura quickly rolls away from her attacker. Then she grabs a pillow and holds it up to cover her nakedness. Montes thrashes about in a futile attempt to free himself from Moncrief and the cop. He keeps struggling and manages to push his one free hand under another pillow. He pulls out a pistol. He shoots it once. The bullet hits the TV screen. It shatters into a small mountain of glass pieces. Moncrief pushes his own index and middle fingers into Montes's face. The drunken Montes manages to get off one more shot. The bullet hits a Vice officer's forearm. As Moncrief and the two officers struggle to pull the naked fat man to his feet, Montes struggles to bring his arm around. Montes aims the gun at Laura.

A final shot. It comes from Moncrief's gun.

The bullet goes right into Montes's neck via his Adam's apple.

Laura Delarico is sobbing. K. Burke is on her cell, calling for reinforcements, forensics, the coroner, police attorneys, the DA's office. Nick Elliott closes his eyes and shakes his head back and forth.

When she finishes her phone calls, K. Burke takes a gray jumpsuit from one of the police kits. She walks to Laura and helps her slip into it. For just a moment Burke's eyes meet Moncrief's.

The two of them are thinking the same thing. They are no closer to solving the case of Maria Martinez. And the one person who might have helped them is now dead.

CHAPTER 23

PHOTOGRAPHERS. AND MORE PHOTOGRAPHERS. Detectives and more detectives. Statements are made and then repeated. Hotel guests wander into the hallway.

We go to the precinct. More detectives. Two police attorneys. Everyone agrees: my bullet was justified. The surveillance video verifies what happened. My colleagues can easily rationalize that the world is a better place without Paulo Montes. I want to rationalize it also, but I cannot ignore the fact that I'm the cop who made it happen.

I go home.

"I'm awake," I hear Dalia shout. "Be right out."

I move toward the bedroom.

We meet in the hallway, and we stand directly in front of a black-and-white Léger poster, a drawing of four people artfully intertwined. Dalia and I do not kiss, but we hug each other with all our strength, as if we are afraid that the other person might slip away.

A few minutes later we are seated on a sofa. We watch the city sky slowly brighten. We both sip a snifter of Rémy. I devour a bowl of cashews. I tell her about my evening. Her face fills with horror, her eyes widen when I tell her about the horrific ending.

"Oh, my God, Luc. You must feel…I don't know…I don't know how you must feel."

"I don't think I know, either," I say. "I've never killed anyone."

I find myself remembering the shooting range near Porte de la Chapelle, where I spent so many hours learning how to load and shoot, load and shoot. The paper dummies, the foolishly big ear protectors. One-handed aim, two-handed aim, shoot from a prone position, shoot from a standing position. But shoot, always shoot. You got him. You got him. You missed him. You got him.

My plan for Montes would have worked. I am sure it would have worked.

I take the last gulp of my Cognac. I swipe the inside of the cashew bowl with my index finger. I touch my salty finger to the tip of Dalia's tongue. She smiles. I hold her tightly.

I tell Dalia that all I want to do now is sleep. She understands. We begin walking toward the bedroom. I stop for a moment. So Dalia stops also.

I have an idea. A very good idea. So good I want to share it with someone. But I'd be a fool to share it with Burke and Elliott. What about Dalia? I usually tell her everything, but not this time, not this idea. She'd kill me if she knew.

Dalia looks up at me.

"You're smiling," she says. "What are you thinking about?"

"Just you," I say. And as we fall on the bed, I consider crossing my fingers behind my back.

CHAPTER 24

I CALL GARY KUEHN at Vice. He's one of the few guys in that department who's smart enough to appreciate what he calls my shenanigans.

Shenanigans. English is a wonderful language.

Gary e-mails me a list of names of "superior sex workers" (translation: high-class hookers) and their managers (translation: drug-dealing abusive johns). I specifically request names of girls who regularly service the toniest areas of the Upper East Side.

I tell my new plan to no one—not K. Burke, not Nick Elliott, not even Gary. At midafternoon, I take an Uber car across town and check into a room at the Pierre, on Fifth Avenue at 61st Street. A mere seventeen hundred dollars a night. I silently thank my father for the large allowance that makes this expensive escapade possible.

I arrange for a series of these high-priced call girls to visit my room—one girl every thirty minutes. I do all the scheduling—the phoning and texting and e-mailing—myself.

At three o'clock a girl with incandescent mahogany skin appears. Her skin is so shiny it looks polished. Her hair is short and dark. She smiles. I am sitting in a comfortable blue club chair. She approaches me and touches my face.

"Please have a seat over there," I say, pointing to the identical blue club chair opposite my own. No doubt she thinks we're about to begin a freaky fantasy.

"Here is the first piece of news: I'm not going to touch you, but I will, of course, pay you for this visit." I hand her three hundred-dollar bills. (The agreed-upon price was two fifty.)

"Here is the second piece of news, and perhaps it is not quite so welcome. I am going to ask you some questions."

She smiles. I quickly add, "Nothing uncomfortable—just some simple talking and chatting. I am a detective with the NYPD."

Her face becomes a mask of fear.

"But I promise. You have nothing to worry about."

The questions begin:

Have you ever serviced a client at 655 Park Avenue?

Have you ever serviced a client at the Auberge du Parc Hotel?

Have you ever serviced a client who acted with extreme violence?

A client who hurt you, threatened you, brandished a weapon, a gun, a cane, a stick, a whip? A client who tried to slip a tablet or a powder or a suspicious liquid into a beverage?

Have you ever met with a client who was famous in his field—an actor, a diplomat, a senator, a governor, a foreign leader, a clergyman?

The answers are all no. And the pattern remains the same for every woman who follows.

A few of them tell me about men with some odd habits, but as the woman in the tight yellow jeans says, "A lot of guys have odd habits. That's why they go to prostitutes. Maybe their fancy wives don't want to suck toes or fuck in a tennis skirt or take it up the ass."

Other statements are made.

A tall woman, the only woman I've ever seen who looked beautiful in a Mohawk haircut, says, "Okay, there is this congressman from New Jersey that I see once or twice a month."

A very tan woman in a saronglike outfit says, "Yeah, one guy was *sort of* into whips, but all he wanted was for me to unpin my hair and swing it against his dick."

A woman who shows up in blue shorts cut off at mid-thigh, her shirt tied just above the navel, gives me some hope, but she, too, is a waste of time. "I think I was at 655 Park once. But it was for a woman. I hate working chicks. The few I've done were all, like, just into kissing and touching and petting. They're more work than the guys."

No information of any value. Yes, two of the girls have been slapped—both of them by men who were drunk. Yes, the girl-on-girl prostitute at 655 Park works for the Russian gang, but she knows nothing about the death of Maria Martinez, and she has never even heard of Paulo Montes.

What I am learning from these few hours of wasted interviews is the knowledge that the world is filled with men who are happy to pay to get laid. That's it. That's the deal. Over and out. It is a gross and humiliating way for a girl to make money, but, in most cases, each has made her separate peace with it.

The interviews end. Thousands of dollars later I have nothing to show for my work.

It is definitely time for me to leave the Pierre.

It is definitely time for me to return home to Dalia.

CHAPTER 25

EVERY MORNING AT THE precinct, K. Burke and I have the following dialogue.

Instead of saying the words "Good morning," she looks at me and says sternly, "You're late."

I always respond with a cheery "And good morning to you, *ma belle.*"

It has become a funny little routine between the two of us, the sort of thing two friends might do. Who knows? Maybe K. Burke and I are becoming friends. Sometimes a mutually miserable situation can bring people together.

But this morning it's different. She greets me by saying, "Don't bother sitting down, Moncrief. We have an assignment from Inspector Elliott."

All I know is that unless Elliott has had an unexpected stroke of genius (highly unlikely) I am not interested in the assignment. I must also face the fact that my mood is terrible: interviewing the call girls has led to absolutely nothing, and I can share my frustration with no one. If I were to tell Burke or Elliott about my unapproved tactic they would both be furious.

"Whatever it is the inspector wants, we'll do it later."

"It's already later," Burke says. "It's one o'clock in the afternoon. Let's go."

"Go where? It's lunchtime. I'm thinking that fish restaurant on 49th Street. A bit of sole meunière and a crisp bottle of Chablis…"

"Stop being a Frenchman for just one minute, Moncrief," she says.

I can tell that K. Burke is uncomfortable with what she's about to say, but out it comes: "He wants us to visit some high-class strip clubs. He's even done some of the grunt work for us. He's compiled a list of clubs. Take a look at your phone."

I swipe the screen and click on my assignments folder. I see a page entitled "NYC Club Visits. From: N. Elliott."

Sapphire, 333 East 60th Street
Rick's Cabaret, 50 West 33rd Street
Hustler Club, 641 West 51st Street

Three more places are listed after these.

As a young man in Paris, full of booze and often with a touch of cocaine in my nose, I would occasionally visit the Théâtre Chochotte, in Saint-Germain-des-Prés, with some pals. It was not without its pleasures, but on one such visit I had a very bad experience: I ran into my father and my uncle in the VIP lounge. That was the night I crossed Chochotte and all Parisian strip clubs off my list. Even a son who has a much better relationship than I have with my father does not ever want to end up in a strip joint with the old man.

As for clubs in New York…I am no longer a schoolboy. I am no longer touching my nose with cocaine. And I now have Dalia waiting at home for me.

The fact is that my assignment would be the envy of most of my colleagues. But I am weary and frustrated and pissed off and…it seems impossible for me to believe, but I am growing tired of so much female flesh in my face.

"I won't do it," I say to Burke. "You do it alone. I'll stay here and do some detail analysis."

"No way am I going alone, Moncrief. C'mon."

"I cannot. I will not," I say.

"Then I suggest you tell that to Inspector Elliott."

I feel my whole heart spiraling downward. The entrapment with Laura. The death of Paulo. The futile interviews with the call girls. Now I am expected to go to these sad places, where a glass of cheap vodka costs thirty dollars, and try to talk to women with breast implants who are sliding up and down poles.

"I am sick. I am tired," I tell Burke.

"I know you are," Burke says. And I can tell she means it. "But you need to do it for Maria. This is—"

I snap at her. "I do not need a pep talk. I know you're trying to be helpful, but that kind of thing doesn't work with me."

Burke just stares at me.

"Tell Inspector Elliott we will make these 'visits' tomorrow. Maria will still be dead tomorrow. Right now, I'm going home."

CHAPTER 26

BURKE WILL TELL ELLIOTT that I went home because of illness. And, of course, Elliott won't believe it.

But I think that K. Burke and I are now simpatico enough for her to cover for me.

"Suddenly he's sick?" Elliott will say. "That's pure bullshit."

The answer Burke might produce could go something like, "Well, he was out sick all day yesterday."

It makes no difference. For the moment I am engaged in a very important project: I am in a store on Ninth Avenue selecting two perfect fillets of Dover sole. The cost at Seabreeze Fish Market for a pound of this beautiful fish is one hundred and twenty dollars. I have no trouble spending that much (or more) on a bottle of wine. But—Jesus!—this is fish. In the taxi uptown to Dalia's apartment I hold the package of fish as if it were a newborn infant being brought home from the hospital.

The moment I walk through the door of the apartment I feel lighter, better, stronger. It's as if the air in Dalia's place is purer than the air in the dangerous, depressing crime scenes I frequent.

I place the precious fish in the refrigerator.

I unpack the few other items I've bought and remove my shirt. I'm feeling better already.

In a moment I'll start chopping the shallots, chopping the parsley, and heating the wine for the mustard sauce. This preparation is what trained chefs call the *mise en place*.

I decide to take off my suit pants. I toss them on the chair where my shirt is resting. I am—in my mind—no longer in a professionally equipped kitchen overlooking Central Park. I am in a wonderfully sunny beach house on the Côte d'Azur. I am no longer a gloomy angry detective; I am a young tennis pro away for a week of rest, awaiting the arrival of his luscious girlfriend.

I press a button on the entertainment console. Suddenly the music blares. It is Dalia's newest favorite: Selena Gomez. "Me and the Rhythm." I sing along, creating my own lyrics to badly match whatever Selena is singing.

Ooh, all the rhythm takes you over.

I chop the shallot to the beat of the music. I scrape the chopped pieces into my hand and toss them into a sauté pan.

I am moving my feet and hips. I drop a half pound of Irish butter into the pan, and now I feel almost compelled to dance.

I sing. I dance. When I don't sing I am talking to an imaginary Dalia.

"Yes," I am saying. *"Your favorite. Dover sole."*

"Yes, there is a bottle of Dom Pérignon already in the fridge."

"Yes, I left early to make this dinner."

"The hell with them. They can fire me, then."

The music beats on. I rhythmically slap away at the parsley leaves with my chef's knife.

In the distance I hear the buzzing of a cell phone. The sound of the phone at first seems to be a part of Selena's song. Then I recognize the tone. It is my police phone. For a moment I consider ignoring it. Then I think that perhaps there is news on Maria Martinez's case. Or it might merely be Nick or K. Burke calling to torment me. But nothing can torment me tonight.

I let the music continue. Whoever my caller is can sing along with me.

I yank my suit jacket from the pile of clothing. I find my phone.

Ooh, all the rhythm takes you over.

"What's up?" I yell loudly above the music.

My prediction is correct. It is Inspector Elliott on the line.

He speaks. I listen. I stop dancing. I drop the phone. I fall to my knees and I scream.

"Noooooooo!"

CHAPTER 27

BUT THE TRUTH IS "yes." There has been another woman stabbed, another woman connected to the New York City police. Only this time the woman is neither an officer nor a detective. This time the woman is also connected to me.

"Who is it, goddamn it?"

Elliott's exact words: "It's Dalia, Moncrief."

A pause and then he adds quietly, *"Dalia is dead."*

I kneel on the gray granite floor and pound it. Tears do not come, but I cannot stop saying "no." If I say the word loudly enough, often enough, it will eradicate the fact of "yes."

For a few moments I actually believe that the call from Nick Elliott never happened. I am on the floor, and I pick up the phone. I observe it as if it were a foreign object—a paperweight, a tiny piece of meteorite, a dead rat. But the caller ID says N/ELLIOTT/NYPD/17PREC.

An overwhelming energy goes through me. Within seconds I am back in my pants and shirt. I slip on my shoes, without socks. I go bounding out the door, and the madness within me makes me certain that running down the back stairs of the apartment building will be faster than calling for the elevator.

Once outside, I see two officers waiting in a patrol car.

"Detective Moncrief. We're here to take you to the crime scene. Take the passenger seat."

I don't even know where the crime scene is. I grab the shoulders of the other cop and shake him violently.

"Where the hell are you taking me? Where is she?" I shout. "Where are we going?"

"To 235 East 20th Street, sir. Please get into the car."

Within moments we are suffocated in midtown rush-hour traffic. How can there be so much traffic when Dalia is dead?

At Seventh Avenue and 45th, the streets are thick with sightseeing buses and cabs. Some people are dressed up as Big Bird and Minnie Mouse. The sidewalks teem with tourists and druggies and strollers and women in saris and schoolchildren on trips and…I tell the driver to unlock the doors. I will walk, run, fly.

"This traffic will break below 34th Street, Detective."

"Unlock the fucking door!" I scream. And so he does, and I am on the sidewalk again. I don't give a shit that I am pushing people aside.

Within minutes I am at Seventh Avenue and 34th Street. The streets remain packed with people and cabs and cars and buses.

I cross against the light at 34th Street, Herald Square, Macy's. Where the hell is Santa Claus when you need him?

Sirens. Cars jostle to clear a route for the vehicle screeching out the sirens.

I am rushing east on 32nd Street. I am midway between Broadway and Fifth Avenue, a block packed almost entirely, crazily, with Korean restaurants. Suddenly the sirens are fiercely loud.

"Get in the car, Moncrief. Get back in the car." It is the same driver of the same patrol car that picked me up earlier. They were right about the traffic, but I am vaguely glad that I propelled myself this far.

In a few minutes we are at 235 East 20th Street. The police academy of the New York City Police Department. The goddamn police academy. Dalia is dead at the police academy. How the hell did she end up here?

"We're here, Detective," says one of the officers.

I turn my head toward the building. K. Burke is walking quickly toward the car. Behind her is Nick Elliott. My chest hurts. My throat burns.

Dalia is dead.

CHAPTER 28

"THIS WAY, LUC," K. Burke says. Both Burke and Nick Elliott guide me by the elbows down a corridor—painted cement blocks, an occasional bulletin board, a fire-alarm box, a fire-extinguisher case.

The usual cast of characters is standing nearby: police officers, forensics, the coroner's people, two firemen, some young people— probably students—carrying laptops and water bottles. A very large sign is taped to a wall at the end of the corridor. It is a photograph of four people: a white male officer, an Asian female officer, a black male officer, a white female officer. Above the big grainy photo are big grainy blue letters:

SERVE WITH DIGNITY. SERVE WITH COURAGE.
THE NEW YORK CITY POLICE DEPARTMENT

Burke and Elliott steer me into a large old-fashioned lecture hall. The stadium seating ends at the bottom with a large table at which a lecturer usually stands. Behind it are a video screen and a green chalkboard. In this teaching pit also stand two officers and two doctors from the chief medical examiner's office. On the side aisles are other officers, other detectives, and, as we descend closer to the bottom of that aisle, a gurney on which a body rests.

K. Burke speaks to me as we reach the gurney. She is saying something to me, but I can't hear her. I am not hearing anything. I am just staring straight ahead as a doctor pulls back the gauzy sheet from Dalia's head and shoulders.

"The wound was in the stomach, sir," she says.

She knows I need no further details at the moment.

Need I say that Dalia looks exquisite? Perfect hair. Perfect eyelashes. A touch of perfect makeup. Perfect. Just perfect. Just fucking unbelievably perfect.

How can she be so beautiful and yet dead?

In my mind I am still screaming "No!" but I say nothing.

I look away from her, and I see the others in the room backing away, looking away, trying to give me privacy in a very public situation.

I must touch Dalia. I should do it gently, of course. I take Dalia's face in both my hands. Her cheeks feel cold, hard. I lean in and brush my lips against her forehead. I pull back a tiny bit to look at her. Then I lean in again to kiss her on the lips.

The room is silent. Deadly silent. I have heard silence before. But the world has never been this quiet.

I will stand here for the rest of my life just looking at her. Yes, that's what I'll do. I'll never move from this spot. I stroke her hair. I touch her shoulders. I stand erect, then turn around.

Nick Elliott is looking at the ground. K. Burke's chin is quivering. Her eyes are wet. I speak, perhaps to Nick or K. Burke or everyone in the room or perhaps I am simply talking to myself.

"Dalia is dead."

CHAPTER 29

"DO YOU WANT TO ride in the ambulance with her?" Elliott asks. And before I can answer he adds, "I'll go with you if you want. We've got to get Dalia to the research area."

The research area. That is the NYPD euphemism for "the morgue." It is what they say to parents whose child has been run over by a drunk driver.

"No," I say. "There's nothing to be done."

K. Burke looks at me and says what everybody says in a situation like this: "I don't know what to say."

And me? I don't know what to say, either—or what to think or feel or do. So I say what comes to mind: "Keep me posted."

I walk quickly through the lineup of colleagues and strangers lining the cement-block hallway. I jump over the giant stone barricades that encircle the police academy in case of attack. I am now running up Third Avenue.

"May I help you, monsieur?" That is the voice I hear. Where have I run? I don't recall a destination. I barely remember running. Did I leave Dalia's dead body behind? I look at the woman who just spoke to me. She used the word *monsieur.* Am I in Paris?

She is joined by a well-dressed man, an older man, a gentleman.

"Can I be of some help, Monsieur Moncrief?"

"Où suis-je?" I ask. Where am I?

"Hermès, Monsieur Moncrief. Bonsoir. Je peux vous aider?"

The Hermès store on Madison Avenue. It is…was…Dalia's favorite place in the entire world to shop.

"Non. Merci, Monsieur. Je regarde." Just looking.

On the glass shelves is a collection of handbags, purses, and pocketbooks in red and yellow and green. Like Easter and Christmas. I feel calm amid the beauty. It is a museum, a palace, a château. The silk scarves hanging from golden hooks. The glass cases of watches and cufflinks. The shelves of briefcases and leather shopping bags. And then the calm inside me dissipates. I say, *"Bonsoir et merci"* to the sales associate.

I have neither my police phone nor my personal cell. I do not have my watch. I do not know the time. I know I am not crazy. I'm simply crazed.

It's early evening. I walk to Fifth Avenue. The sidewalks are crowded, and the shops are open. I walk down to the Pierre. I was recently inside the Pierre. Was I? I think I was. I continue walking south, toward the Plaza. No water in the fountain? A water shortage, perhaps? I turn east, back toward Madison Avenue, then start north again.

Bottega Veneta. I walk inside. No warm greeting here. A bigger store than Hermès. Instead of a symphony of leather in color, this is a muted place in grays and blacks and many degrees of brown. Calming, calming, calming, until it is calming no longer.

I leave. My next stop is Sherry-Lehmann, the museum of wine. I

walk to the rear of the store, where they keep their finest bottles—
the Romanée-Conti, Pétrus, Le Pin, Ramonet Montrachet, the
thousand-dollar Moët. The bottles should all be displayed under
glass, like the diamonds at Tiffany.

I am out on the sidewalk again. I am afraid that if I don't keep
moving, I will explode or collapse. It is that extraordinary feeling
that nothing good will ever happen again.

A no-brainer: I cannot return to Dalia's apartment at 15 Central Park West. Instead I will go to the loft where I once lived. The
place is in the stupidly chic Meatpacking District. I bought the loft
before I renewed my life with Dalia. I sometimes lend the place to
friends from Europe who are visiting New York. I'm pretty sure it
is empty right now.

Will I pick up the pieces? There is no way that will ever happen.

Move on, they will say. Mourn, then move on. I will not do
that, because I can't.

Get over it? Never. Someone else? Never.

Nothing will ever be the same.

As I give the address to the cabdriver, I find my chest heaving
and hurting. I insist—I don't know why—on holding in the tears.
In those few minutes, with my chest shaking and my head aching, I
realize what Elliott and Burke and probably others have come to realize: first, my partner, Maria Martinez; then my lover, Dalia Boaz.

Oh, my God. This isn't about prostitutes. This isn't about
drugs. This is about me.

Somebody wants to hurt me. And that somebody has suc-
ceeded.

CHAPTER 30

A LOFT. A BIG space; bare, barren. Not a handsome space. It is way too basic to be anything but big.

I lived here before Dalia came back into my life. Even when I lived here, I was too compulsive to have allowed it to become a cheesy bachelor pad—no piles of dirty clothing; no accumulation of Chinese-food containers. In fact, no personal touches of any kind. But of course I was spending too many of my waking hours with the NYPD to think about furniture and paint and bathroom fixtures.

I turn the key and walk inside. I am almost startled by the sparseness of it—a gray sofa, a black leather club chair, a glass dining table where no one has ever eaten a meal. Some old files are stacked against a wall. Empty shelves near the sofa. Empty shelves in the kitchen. I have lived most of my New York life with Dalia, at Dalia's home. That was my real home. Where am I now?

I stretch out on the sofa. Fifteen seconds later, I am back on my feet. The room is stuffy, dry, hot. I walk to the thermostat that will turn on the air-conditioning, but I stare at the controls as if I don't quite know how to adjust the temperature. I remember that there is a smooth single-malt Scotch in a cabinet near the entryway, but why bother? I need to use the bathroom, but I just don't have energy enough to walk to the far side of the loft.

Then the buzzer downstairs rings.

At least I think it's the buzzer downstairs. It's been so long since I heard it. I walk to the intercom. The buzz comes again, then once more. Then I remember what I'm expected to say. A phrase that is ridiculously simple.

"Who is it?"

For a split second I stupidly imagine that it will be Dalia. "It was a terrible joke," she will say with a laugh. "Inspector Elliott helped me fool you."

Now a hollow voice comes from the intercom.

"It's K. Burke."

I buzz her inside. Moments later I open the door and let her into the loft.

"How did you know where to find me?" I ask.

"I called your cell twenty times. You never picked up. Then I called Dalia's place twenty times. You weren't there, *or* you weren't picking up. So I found this place listed as the home address in your HR file. If I didn't find you here, I was going to forget it. But I got lucky."

"No, K. Burke. *I got lucky.*"

I have no idea why I said something so sweet. But I think I mean it. Again, an idea that comes and goes in a split second: whoever is trying to destroy me—will he go after K. Burke next?

She gives me a smile. Then she says, "I'm about to say the thing that always annoys me when other people say it."

"And that is…"

"Is there anything I can do for you?"

I take a deep breath.

"You mean like brewing a pot of coffee or bringing me a bag of doughnuts or cleaning my bathroom or finding the son of a bitch who—"

"Okay, I got it," she says. "I understand. But actually, Nick Elliott and I did do something for you."

My forehead wrinkles, and I say, "What?"

"We tracked down Dalia's father. He's in Norway shooting a film."

"I was going to call him soon," I say. "But I was building up courage. Thank you." And just thinking about father and daughter begins to break my already severed heart.

"How did he accept the news?" As if I needed to ask.

"It was awful. He wailed. He screamed. He put his assistant on, and he eventually…well, he sort of composed himself and got back on the line."

My eyes begin filling with tears. My chin quivers. I rub my eyes. I am not trying to hide my emotions. I am merely trying to get through them.

"He sends you his love," K. Burke says. I nod.

"He is as fine a man as Dalia was a woman," I say.

"He asked me to tell you two things."

I can't imagine what Monsieur Boaz wanted to tell me.

"He said, 'Tell Luc that I will come to America tomorrow, but he should bury Dalia as soon as possible. That is the Jewish way.'"

"I understand," I say. Then I ask, "And the other?"

"He said, 'Tell Luc thank you...for taking such good care of my girl.'"

This comment should make me weep, but instead I explode with anger. Not at Menashe Boaz, but at myself.

"That's not true!" I yell. "I did *not* take good care of her."

"Of course it's true," K. Burke says firmly. "You loved her totally. Everybody knows that."

"I...let...her...die."

"That's just stupid, Moncrief. And it smells a little of..." K. Burke abruptly stops talking.

"What? Finish your thought. It smells of what?" I say.

"It smells of...well...self-pity. Dalia was murdered. You could not have prevented it."

I walk to the floor-to-ceiling windows of the loft. I look down at Gansevoort Street. It's this year's chic hot-cool place to be—the expensive restaurants and expensive boutiques, the High Line, the cobblestone streets. It is packed with people. I am disgusted with them because I am disgusted with me. Because Dalia and I will never again be among those people.

I turn and face Detective Burke, and suddenly I am more peaceful. I am truly grateful that she is here. She has stopped by to offer the "personal touch" and I was hesitant at first. Afraid I would feel nervous or embarrassed. But K. Burke has done a good thing.

I walk back toward her and speak slowly, carefully.

"There is one thing we need to discuss very soon. You must realize that these two murders had nothing to do with prostitutes or

Brazilian drug dealers or…well, all the things we have been guessing at."

"I realize that," she says. I continue speaking.

"The first murder, at a rich man's home, was to confuse us. The next murder, at a school where people learn to be police professionals—that was to torment us."

K. Burke nods in simple agreement.

"These murders have to do with *me*," I say.

"In that case," K. Burke says, "these murders have to do with *us*."

CHAPTER 31

"WHAT THE HELL IS the story with these two murders?"

This question keeps exploding off the walls of NYPD precincts. It is the commissioner's question. It is Nick Elliott's question. And—obsessively, interminably, awake or asleep—it is my question.

The question is asked a thousand times, and a thousand times the answer comes back the same.

"No idea. Just no goddamn idea."

Forensics brought in nothing. Surveillance cameras showed us nothing. Interviews at the scene turned up nothing.

So it is now time for me to do the only thing left to do: turn inward and rely entirely on my instincts. They have helped me in the past, and they have failed me, too. But instinct is all I have left.

I confront Nick Elliott. I tell him that the answer to the murders is obviously not in New York. The answer must be in Paris.

"Paris?" he shouts.

Then I say, "I need to go to Paris—look around, nose around, see if I can find something there."

Nick Elliott gives it a long pause and then says, "Maybe that's not a bad idea."

Then I tell him that I want to take K. Burke with me.

He pauses again, another long pause. Then he speaks. "Now, *that's* a bad idea."

"Inspector, this is no holiday I'm planning. This is work. K. Burke and I will be examining cases that—"

"Okay, okay, let me think about it," Elliott says. "Maybe it'll help. On the other hand, it might end up being a waste of time and money."

I think quickly and say, "Then it will be a waste of *my* time and *my* money. I'll supply the money for the trip. I only care about getting to the bottom of these murders."

"I guess so," says Elliott.

I say, "I'll take that as a yes."

A minute later I am telling K. Burke to go home and pack.

Her reaction? "I've never been to Paris."

My reaction? "Why am I not surprised?"

CHAPTER 32

K. BURKE AND I are sitting at a steel desk in a small room with bad Internet service at Les Archives de la Préfecture de Police, the dreary building on the periphery of Paris where all the old police records are kept. Here you can examine every recorded police case since the end of the Great War. Here you can discover the names of the French collaborators during the Vichy regime. You can examine the records of the Parisian bakers who have been accused of using tainted yeast in their bread. Here are the records of the thousands of murders, assaults, knife attacks, shootings, and traffic violations that have occurred in the past hundred years in the City of Light.

It is also here that K. Burke and I hope to find some small (or, better yet, large) clue that could connect us to whoever is responsible for the brutal deaths of Maria Martinez and my beloved Dalia.

To find the person who wishes to hurt me so deeply.

"Here," says Detective Burke, pointing to my name on the screen of the archive's computer. *"L. Moncrief était responsable…"*

I translate: "L. Moncrief was responsible for the evidence linking the Algerian diplomat to the cartel posing as Dominican priests in the 15th arrondissement."

I press a computer key and say to Burke, "Listen: after years of being dragged to church by my mother, I know a real priest when I see one, and no *prêtre* I'd ever seen had such a well-groomed beard and mustache. Then I noticed that his shoes…eh, never mind. See what's next."

We study my other cases. Some of those I worked on are ridiculously small—a Citroën stolen because the owner left the keys in the ignition; a lost child who stopped for a free *jus d'orange* on his way home from school; a homeless man arrested for singing loudly in a public library.

Other cases are much more significant. Along with the phony Dominicans, there was the drug bust in Pigalle, the case I built my reputation on. But there was also a gruesome murder in Montmartre, on rue Caulaincourt, during which a pimp's hands and feet were amputated.

In this last case my instincts led me to a pet cemetery in Asnières-sur-Seine. Both the severed hands and feet were found at the grave of the pimp's childhood pet, a spaniel. Instinct.

But nothing in the police archive is resonating with me. I do not feel, either through logic or instinct, any link from these past cases and the awful deaths of my two beloved women.

"I think I need another café au lait, Moncrief," K. Burke says. Her eyelids are covering half her eyes. Jet lag has definitely attacked her.

"What you need is a taxi back to Le Meurice," I say. "It is now *quatorze heures*.…"

K. Burke looks confused.

I translate. "Two o'clock in the afternoon."

"Gotcha," she says.

"Go back to the hotel. Take a nap, and I will come knocking on your door at *dix-sept heures.* Forgive me. I will come knocking at five o'clock."

I add, "Good-bye, K. Burke."

"Au revoir," she says. Her accent makes me cringe, then smile.

"You see?" I add. "You're here just seven hours, and already you're on your way to becoming a true *Parisienne.*"

CHAPTER 33

WE MEET AT FIVE.

"I am not a happy man," I say to K. Burke after I give our destination to the cabdriver. Then I say, "Perhaps I will never be a completely happy man again, but I am *un peu content* when I am in Paris." Burke says nothing for a few seconds.

"Perhaps someday you will be happi*er*." She speaks with an emphasis on the last syllable. Perhaps someday I will be.

Then I explain to her that because we will have to get back to our investigation tomorrow—"And, like many things, it might come to a frustrating end," I caution—this early evening will be the only chance for me to show her the glory of Paris.

Then I quickly add, "But not the Eiffel Tower or the Louvre or Notre Dame. You can see those on your own. I will show you the special places in Paris. Places that are visited by only the very wise and the very curious."

Detective Burke says, *"Merci, Monsieur Moncrief."*

I smile at her, and then I say to the cabdriver, *"Nous sommes arrivés."* We are here.

Burke reads the sign on the building aloud. Her accent is amusingly American-sounding: "Museé…des…Arts…Forains?"

"It is the circus museum," I say. And soon we are standing in a huge warehouse that holds the forty carousels and games and bright neon signs that a rich man thought were worth preserving.

"I can't decide whether this is a dream or a nightmare," Burke says.

"I think that it is *both*."

We ride a carousel that whirls amazingly fast. "I feel like I'm five again!" shouts K. Burke. We play a game that involves plaster puppets and cloth-covered bulls. K. Burke wins the game. Then we are out and on our way again.

This time out I tell our cabdriver to take us to Paris Descartes University.

"Vous êtes médecin?" the cabdriver asks.

I tell him that my companion and I are doctors of crime, which seems both to surprise and upset him. A few minutes later we are ascending in the lift to view the Musée d'Anatomie Delmas-Orfila-Rouvière. The place is almost crazier than the circus museum. It's a medical museum with hundreds of shelves displaying skulls and skeletons and wax models of diseased human parts. It is at once astonishing and disgusting.

At one point Burke says, "We're the only people here."

"You need special permission to enter."

"Aren't we the lucky ones?" Burke says, with only slight sarcasm.

From there we take another cab ride—to the Pont des Arts, a pedestrian bridge across the Seine. I show her the "love locks," the thousands of small padlocks attached to the rails of the bridge by lovers.

"They are going to relocate some of the locks," I tell Burke. "There are so many that they fear the bridge may collapse."

So much love, I think. And for a moment my heart hurts. But then I hail another cab. I point out the Pitié-Salpêtrière hospital, and we both laugh when I explain that it was once an asylum for "hysterical women."

"Don't get any ideas, Moncrief," Burke says.

Since our bodies are still on American time, it is almost lunchtime for us, and I ask K. Burke if she is hungry.

"Tu as faim?" I ask.

"*Très, très* hungry. Famished, in fact."

Ten minutes later, we are in the rough-and-tumble Pigalle area. I tell Detective Burke that she can always dine at the famous Parisian restaurants—Taillevent, Guy Savoy, even the dining room in our hotel. But tonight, I am taking her to my favorite restaurant, Le Petit Canard.

"Isn't this the area where you made your famous drug bust?" Burke asks.

"C'est vrai," I tell her. "You have a good memory."

She is looking out the taxi window. The tourists have disappeared from the streets. The artists must be inside smoking weed. Only vagrants and prostitutes are hanging around.

"Ignore the neighborhood. Le Petit Canard is amazing. I used to come here a great deal when I lived in Paris. With friends, with my father, with…"

She says, "With Dalia, I'm sure." She pauses and says, "I am so sorry for you, Moncrief. So sorry."

Softly, I mutter, "Thank you."

Then I add, "And thank you for allowing me to take you to the crazy tourist sights. It lifted my spirits. It made me feel a little better, Katherine."

Burke appears slightly startled. We both realize that for the first time I have called Detective Burke by her proper first name.

I look closely at Burke's face, a lovely face, a face that goes well with such a lovely evening in such a beautiful city.

"Okay," I say loudly and with great heartiness. "Let me call for the wine list, and we shall begin. We will enjoy a glorious dinner tonight."

I fake an overly serious sad face, a frown. "Because you know that tomorrow…*retour au travail*. Do you know what those three French words mean?"

"I'm afraid so," she says. "'Back to work.'"

CHAPTER 34

MONCRIEF AND K. BURKE return to the hotel. If you were unaware of the details of their relationship, you would assume that they were just another rich and beautiful couple strolling through the ornate lobby of the Meurice.

Much to Moncrief's surprise and pleasure, K. Burke had brought along an outfit that was quite chic—a long white shirt over which hung a gray cashmere sweater. That sweater fell over a black slim skirt. It was finished with short black boots. Burke could *possibly* pass as a fashionable Parisian, and she could *certainly* pass as a fashionable American. Moncrief had told her how "snappy" she looked.

"You look snappy yourself, Moncrief," she had said to him. This was, of course, true: a black Christian Dior suit with a slight sheen to it; a white shirt with a deep burgundy-colored tie.

Moncrief walked K. Burke back to her room and said good night. He listened while Burke locked her door behind her. Then he walked to the end of the hallway, to his own room.

It was a dinner between friends, between colleagues. K. Burke had expected nothing more. In fact, K. Burke *wanted* nothing more. It had been a spectacular day—the odd museums, then the extraordinary dinner: foie-gras ravioli, Muscovy duckling with mango sherbet, those wonderful little chocolates that fancy French restaurants always bring you with your coffee (or so Moncrief told her).

The night had turned out to be soothing and fun and friendly. He referred to Dalia a few times, and it was with nostalgia, sadness. But there was no darkness when he reminisced about his late girlfriend.

Now, as Burke unscrews and removes her tiny diamond studs, she wonders: *Can you have such a wonderful time with a charming, handsome man and not think about romance?*

Of course you can, she tells herself. But then again, it's impossible to put a man and a woman together—the electrician who comes to fix the wiring, the traffic cop who stops you for speeding, the attorney who is updating your will—and not consider the possibilities of *What if…at another time…under different conditions…*

Burke removes her shirt and sweater. She sits on the bench at the white wood dressing table and removes her boots. As she massages her toes she shakes her head slowly; she is ashamed that she is even having such thoughts. Despite the pleasant dinner, she knows that Moncrief has not remotely begun to recover from Dalia's awful, sudden, horrible death. *And yet here I am, selfishly thinking of how great we look together, like one of those beautiful couples in a perfume ad.*

"Enough nonsense." She actually says these two words out loud. Then she goes into the bathroom, removes her makeup, brushes her teeth, and takes the two antique combs out of her hair. She slips her T-shirt (GO RANGERS) over her head, then she removes her contact lenses and drops them into solution. There is only one more thing to do.

She goes to her pocketbook to do what she does instinctively every night before bed: check the safety on her service weapon. Then she remembers—she doesn't have a gun. The French police said that she and Moncrief were on official business for New York, *not* for Paris. No firearms permits would be issued.

She remembers what Moncrief said to her when she complained.

"Do you feel naked without your gun, K. Burke?"

"No," she had answered. "Just a little underdressed."

CHAPTER 35

THE SAME CRAMPED AND ugly little room. The same primitive air-conditioning. The same stale air. The same inadequate Internet service. But most of all, the same rotten luck in finding "the finger-print," the instinctive connection between one of my past investigations and the tragedies in New York.

Detective Burke and I keep working. We are once again seated in the police archives building, outside Paris. We have been studying the screen so intently that we decided to invest in a shared bottle of eyedrops.

The screen scrolls through old cases, some of which I had actually forgotten—a molestation case that involved a disgusting pediatrician who was also the father of five children; a case of a government official who, not surprisingly, was collecting significant bribes for issuing false health-inspection reports; a case of race fixing at the Longchamp racecourse.

"This looks bigger than fixing a horse race," she says. "The pages go on forever."

"Print them," I say. "I'll look at them more thoroughly later."

Forty pages come spitting out of the printer. Burke says, "It looks like this was a very complicated case."

"Not really," I say. "No case is ever *that* complicated. Either there's a crime or there isn't. The Longchamp case began with a horse trainer. Marcel Ballard was his name. Not a bad guy, I think, but Ballard was weary of fixing the races. So he fought physically—punching, kicking—with the owner and trainer who were running the fix. *And* Ballard had a knife. *And* Ballard killed the owner and cut the other trainer badly."

K. Burke continues scrolling through the cases on the screen. She does say, "Keep going, Moncrief. I'm listening."

"I met with Ballard's wife. She had a newborn, three months old, their fourth child. So I did her a favor, but not without asking for something in return. I persuaded Ballard to confess to the crime and to help us identify the other trainers who were drugging the horses. He cooperated. So thanks to my intervention—and that of my superiors—he was allowed to plead to a lesser charge. Instead of *homicide volontaire,* he was only charged with—"

"Let me guess," says K. Burke. *"Homicide* in*volontaire.*"

"You are both a legal and linguistic genius, K. Burke."

I grab some of the Longchamp papers and go through them quickly. "I'm glad I did what I did," I say. "Madame Ballard is a good woman."

"And the husband? Is he grateful?" K. Burke asks as she continues to study the screen intensely.

"He has written to me many times in gratitude. But one must keep in mind that he did kill a man."

Burke presses a computer key and begins reading about a drug gang working out of Saint-Denis.

"What does this mean, Moncrief? *Logement social.*"

"In New York they call it public housing. A group of heroin dealers had set up a virtual drug supermarket in the basement there. Once I realized that some of our Parisian detectives were involved in the scheme, it was fairly easy—but frightening—to bust."

"How'd you figure out that your own cops were involved?" she asks.

"I simply *felt* it," I say.

"Of course," she says with a bit of sarcasm. "I should have known."

We continue flipping through the cases on the computer. But like the race fixing and murder at Longchamp, like the drug bust in Saint-Denis, all my former cases seem to be a million miles away from New York. No instinct propelled me. No fingerprint arose.

We studied the cold cases also. The kidnapping of the Ugandan ambassador's daughter (unsolved). The rape of an elderly nun at midnight in the Bois de Boulogne (unsolved, but what in hell was an elderly nun doing in that huge park at midnight?). An American woman with whom I had a brief romantic fling, Callie Hansen, who had been abducted for three days by a notorious husband-and-wife team that we were never able to apprehend. Again, nothing clicked.

We come across a street murder near Moulin Rouge. According to the report on the computer screen, one of the witnesses was a woman named Monica Ansel. Aha! Blaise Ansel had been the owner of Taylor Antiquities, the store on East 71st Street. Could

Monica Ansel be his wife? But Monica Ansel, the woman who witnessed the crime at Moulin Rouge, was seventy-one years old.

"Damn!" I say, and I toss the papers from the Longchamp report to the floor. "I have wasted my time and yours, K. Burke. Plus I have wasted a good deal of money. And what do I have to show for it? *De la merde.*"

Even with her limited knowledge of French, K. Burke is able to translate.

"I agree," she says. "Shit."

CHAPTER 36

K. BURKE SITS OUTDOORS at a small bistro table on rue Vieille du Temple. She is alone. Moncrief had asked if he could be by himself for a while. "I must walk. I must think. Perhaps I must mourn. Do you mind?" Moncrief had said.

"I understand," she said, and she did understand. "I don't need a chaperone."

She sips a glass of strong cider and eats a buckwheat crepe stuffed with ham and Gruyère. It is eight o'clock, a fairly early dinner by French standards. At one table sits a family of German tourists—very blond parents with two very beautiful teenage daughters. At another, an older couple (French, Burke suspects) eating and chewing and drinking slowly and carefully. Finally, there are two young Frenchwomen who appear to be…yes, K. Burke is right…very much in love with each other.

Burke's own heart is still breaking for Moncrief, but she must admit that she is enjoying being alone for a few hours.

Back in her hotel room, she takes a warm bath. A healthy dose of lavender bath oils; a natural sea sponge. Afterward, she dries herself off with the thick white bath sheets and douses herself with a nice dose of the accompanying lavender powder.

She slips on her sleep shirt, and she's about to slide under the sheets when her phone buzzes. A text message.

R U Back in yr room? All is well? Mncrf.

She imagines Moncrief in some mysterious part of Paris, at a zinc bar with a big snifter of brandy. She is thankful for his thoughtfulness.

Yes. K. Burke.

But then, for just a moment she considers her own uneasiness. She simply cannot get used to not having a gun to check. So she does the next best thing: she checks that the door is double-locked. She adjusts the air-conditioning, making the temperature low enough for her to happily snuggle under the thick satin comforter. Within a few minutes she is asleep.

Two hours later, she is wide awake. It is barely past midnight, and Burke is afraid that jet lag is playing games with her sleep schedule. Now she may be up for hours. She takes a few deep breaths. The air makes her feel at least a little better. Maybe she will get back to sleep. Maybe she should use the bathroom. Yes, maybe. Or maybe that will prevent her from falling asleep again. On the other hand…

There is a sound in the room. At first she thinks it's the air conditioner kicking back into gear. Perhaps it is the noise from the busy rue de Rivoli below. She sits up in bed. The noise. Again. Burke realizes now that the sound is coming from the door to her hotel room. Some sort of key? What the hell?

"Who's there?" she shouts.

No answer.

"Who's there?"

Goddamn it. Why doesn't she have a gun?

She should have insisted that Moncrief get them guns. He was right. She feels naked without it.

She rolls quickly—catching herself in the thick covers, afraid in the dark—toward the other side of the bed. She drops to the floor and slides beneath the bed just as a shaft of bright light from the hallway pierces the darkness. Someone else is in the room with her. She moves farther underneath the bed. *Jesus Christ,* she thinks. *This is an awful comedy, a French farce—the woman hiding beneath the bed.*

As soon as she hears the door close, the light from the hallway disappears.

"Don't move, Detective!" a muffled, foreign-sounding voice hisses.

Then a gunshot.

The bullet hits the floor about a foot away from her hand. There's a quick loud snapping sound. A spark on the blue carpet. She tries to move farther under the bed. There is no room. It is so unlike her to not know what to do, to not fight back, to not plot an escape. This feeling of fright is foreign to her.

Another bullet. This one spits its way fiercely through the mattress above her. It hits the floor also.

Another bullet. No spark. No connection.

A groan. A quick thud.

Then a voice.

"K. Burke! It is safe. All is well."

CHAPTER 37

HOTEL MANAGEMENT AND GUESTS in their pajamas almost immediately begin gathering in the hall.

K. Burke emerges from under the bed. We embrace each other the way friends do, friends who have successfully come through a horrible experience together.

"You saved…" she begins. She is shaking. She folds her arms in front of herself. She is working to compose herself.

"I know," I say. I pat her on the back. I am like an old soccer coach with an injured player.

Burke pulls away from me. She blinks—on purpose—a few times, and those simple eye gestures seem to clear her head and calm her nerves. She is immediately back to a completely professional state. She has become the efficient K. Burke I am used to. We both look down at the body. She moves to a nearby closet and wraps herself quickly in a Le Meurice terry-cloth bathrobe.

The dead man fell backwards near the foot of the bed. He wears jeans, a white dress shirt, and Adidas sneakers. His bald head lies in a large and ever-growing pool of blood. It forms a kind of scarlet halo around his face.

The crowd in the hallway seems afraid to enter the room. A

man wearing a blue blazer with LE MEURICE embroidered on the breast pocket appears. He pushes through the crowd. He is immediately followed by two men wearing identical blazers.

I briefly explain what happened, planning to give the police a more detailed story when they arrive.

K. Burke then kneels at the man's head. I watch her touch the man's neck. I can tell by the blood loss, by simply looking at him, that she is merely performing an official act. The guy is gone. Burke stands back up.

"Do you know him, Moncrief?" Burke asks.

"I have never seen him before in my life," I say. "Have you?"

"Of course not," she says. She pauses. Then she says, "He was going to kill me."

"You would have been…the third victim."

She nods. "How did you know that this was happening here, that someone was actually going to break in…threaten my life…try to kill me?"

"Instinct. When I texted you I asked if all was well. So I drank my whiskey.

"But fifteen minutes later, when I am walking back to the hotel, I found myself walking faster and faster, until I was actually running…I just had a feeling. I can't explain it."

"You never can," she says.

CHAPTER 38

THE NEXT MORNING.

Eleven o'clock. I meet K. Burke in the lobby of the hotel.

"So here we are," she says. "Everything is back to *ab*normal."

Even I realize that this is a bad play on words. But it does perfectly describe our situation.

"Look," I say. "A mere apology is unsuitable. I am totally responsible for the near tragedy of last night."

"There's nothing to apologize for. It goes with the territory," she says, but I can see from her red eyes that she did not sleep well. I try to say something helpful.

"I suspect what happened a few hours ago is that the enemy saw us together at some point here in Paris and assumed that we were a couple, which of course we are not."

I realize immediately that my words are insulting, as if it would be impossible to consider us a romantic item. So I speak again, this time more quickly.

"Of course, they might have been correct in the assumption. After all, a lovely-looking woman like you could—"

"Turn it off, Moncrief. I was *not* offended."

I smile. Then I hold K. Burke by the shoulders, look into her weary eyes, and speak.

"Listen. Out of something awful that almost happened last evening...something good has come. I believe I have an insight. I think I may now know the fingerprint of this case."

She asks me to share the theory with her.

"I cannot tell you yet. Not for secrecy reasons, but because I must first be sure, in order to keep my own mind clear. *On y va.*"

"Okay," she says. Then she translates: "Let's go."

We walk outside. I speak to one of the doormen.

"Ma voiture, s'il vous plaît," I say.

"Elle est là, Monsieur Moncrief."

"Your car is here?" Burke asks, and as she speaks my incredibly beautiful 1960 Porsche 356B pulls up and the valet gets out.

"C'est magnifique," Burke says.

The Porsche is painted a brilliantly shiny black. Inside is a custom mahogany instrument panel and a pair of plush black leather seats. I explain to Detective Burke that I had been keeping the car at my father's country house, near Avignon.

"But two days ago I had the car brought up to Paris. And so today we shall use it."

I turn right on the rue de Rivoli, and the Porsche heads out of the city.

After the usual mess of too many people and triple-parked cars and thousands of careless bicycle riders, we are outside Paris, on our way south.

K. Burke twists in her seat and faces me.

"Okay, Moncrief. I have a question that's been bugging me all night."

"I hope to have the answer," I say, trying not to sound anxious.

"The gun that you used last night. Where did you get it?"

I laugh, and with the wind in our hair and the sun in our eyes I fight the urge to throw my head back like an actor in a movie.

"Oh, the gun. Well, when Papa's driver dropped off the car two days ago, I looked in that little compartment, the one in front of your seat, and voilà! Driving gloves, chewing gum, driver's license, and my beautiful antique Nagant revolver. I thought it might come in handy someday."

In the countryside I pick up speed, a great deal of speed. K. Burke does not seem at all alarmed by fast driving. After a few minutes of silence I tell her that I am taking the country roads instead of the A5 *autoroute* so that she might enjoy the summer scenery.

She does not say a word. She is asleep, and she remains so until I make a somewhat sharp right turn at our destination.

K. Burke blinks, rubs her eyes, and speaks.

"Where are we, Moncrief?"

Ahead of us is a long, low, flat gray building. It is big and gloomy. Not like a haunted house or a lost castle. Just a huge grim pile of concrete. She reads the name of the building, carved into the stone.

PRISON CLAIRVAUX

She does a double take.

"What are we doing here, Moncrief?"

"We are here to meet the killer of Maria Martinez and Dalia Boaz."

CHAPTER 39

A FEW YEARS AGO, a detective with the Paris police described the prison at Clairvaux as "hell, but without any of the fun." I think the detective was being kind.

As K. Burke and I present identification to the entrance guards, I tell her, "Centuries ago this was a Cistercian abbey, a place of monks and prayer and chanting."

"Well," she says as she looks around the stained gray walls. "There isn't a trace of God left here."

Burke and I are scanned with an electronic wand, then we step through an X-ray machine and are finally escorted to a large vacant room—no chairs, no tables, no window. We stand waiting a few minutes. The door opens, and an official-looking man as tall as the six-foot doorway enters. He is thin and old. His left eye is made of glass. His name is Tomas Wren. We shake hands.

"Detective Moncrief, I was delighted to hear your message this morning that you would be paying us a visit."

"Merci," I say. "Thank you for accommodating us on such short notice."

Wren looks at Detective Burke and speaks.

"And you, of course, must be Madame Moncrief."

"Non, monsieur, je suis Katherine Burke. Je suis la collègue de Monsieur Moncrief."

"Ah, mille pardons," Wren says. Then Wren turns to me. He is suddenly all business.

"I have told Ballard that you are coming to see him."

"His reaction?" I ask.

"His face lit up."

"I'm glad to hear that," I say.

"You never know with Ballard. He can be a dangerous customer," says Wren. "But he owes you a great deal."

With a touch of levity, I say, "And I owe him a great deal. Without his help I would never have made the arrests that made my career take off."

Wren shrugs, then says, "I have set aside one of the private meeting rooms for you and Mademoiselle Burke," Wren adds.

We follow him down another stained and gray hallway. The private room is small—perhaps merely a dormitory cell from the days of the Cistercian brothers—but it has four comfortable desk chairs around a small maple table. A bit more uninviting, however, are the *bouton d'urgence*—the emergency button—and two heavy metal clubs.

Wren says that he will be back in a moment. "With Ballard," he says.

As soon as Wren exits, Burke speaks.

"I remember this case from the other day, Moncrief. On the computer. Ballard is the horse trainer who killed some guy and wounded another at the Longchamp racecourse."

"Yes, indeed, Detective."

"But I don't totally get what's going on here now."

"You will," I say.

"If you say so," she answers.

I nod, and as I do I feel myself becoming…quiet…no, the proper word is…frightened. A kind of soft anxiety begins falling over me. No man can ever feel happy being in a prison, even for a visit. It is a citadel of punishment and futility. But this is something way beyond simple unhappiness. Burke senses that something is wrong.

"Are you okay, Moncrief?" she says.

"No, I am not. I am twice a widower of sorts. And now I feel I am in the house where those plans were made. No, Detective. I am not okay. But you know what? I don't ever expect to be okay. Excuse me if that sounds like self-pity."

"No need to apologize. I understand."

CHAPTER 40

A CREAKING SOUND, LIKE one you would hear in an old horror movie, comes from the door. It opens, and a burst of light surges into the bleak room.

Wren has returned, and with him is a young prison guard. The guard escorts the prisoner—Marcel Ballard.

Ballard is ugly. His fat face is scarred on both cheeks. Another scar is embedded on the right side of his neck. The three scars show the marks of crude surgical stitching. Prison fights, perhaps?

His head is completely bald. He is unreasonably heavy for a man who dines only on prison rations; he must be trading something of value for extra food.

The guard removes the handcuffs from Ballard.

Ballard comes rushing toward me. He is shouting.

The guard moves to pull Ballard away from me, but Ballard is too fast for him.

"Moncrief, mon ami, mon pote!" he yells. Then he embraces me in a tight bear hug. In accented English, the guard translates, "My friend! My best friend!"

Then Ballard kisses me on both cheeks.

CHAPTER 41

IT IS BALLARD WHO enlightens K. Burke.

"You wonder why we embrace, mademoiselle?"

"Not really," says K. Burke. "I know about you and the detective. I know that you received a lesser sentence because of *him,* and I know that he received some valuable information because of *you.*"

Ballard smiles. I look away from the two of them.

"Detective Moncrief, you have not told your colleague the entire story of our relationship?" Ballard asks, his eyes almost comically wide.

For a reason I can't explain, I am becoming angry. With a snappish tone I respond, "No. I didn't think it was necessary. I thought it was between the two of us."

"But many others know," Ballard responds. "May I tell her?"

"Do whatever you like," I say. The bleakness of the prison, the memory of the Longchamp arrests, and the indelible pain of Maria and Dalia's deaths all close in on me. I am sinking into a depression. There is no reason why I should be angry that Burke will be hearing the story of Ballard and me. Still, he hesitates.

I try to restore a lighter tone to the conversation. "No, really. If you want to tell her, go right ahead."

After a pause, Ballard tells her, "When I was arrested I was the father of an infant, and I was also the father of three other children, all of them under the age of five years."

He pauses, and with a smile says, "Yes, we are a very Catholic family. Four children in five years." Burke does not smile back.

Then he continues. "Life would have been desperate for my wife, Marlene, without me. The children would have starved. When I was sentenced to the two decades in the prison, I worried and prayed, and my prayers were answered.

"In my second month inside this hell, Marlene writes to me with news. She is receiving a monthly stipend, a generous stipend, from Monsieur Moncrief."

He pauses, then adds, "I was overwhelmed with gratitude for his extreme generosity."

Burke nods at Ballard. Then she turns to me and says, "Good man, Detective."

I do not care to slosh around in sentimentality. I gruffly announce, "Look, Ballard. I am here for a reason. An important reason. You may be able to pay me back for that 'extreme generosity.'"

CHAPTER 42

THE GOSSIP NETWORK IN a prison is long and strong.

Ballard confirms this. "I was overcome with sadness and anger when I heard about your police friend and your girlfriend, Detective. I could not write to you. I could not telephone. I did not know what to say. And, I am ashamed to admit, I was afraid. If the other prisoners found out that I was speaking to a member of the Paris police, I might be in danger."

"I understand," I say. "Besides, Marlene wrote me and expressed her outrage and sympathy."

"Très bien," he says. "Marlene is a good woman."

I am silent. I want to speak, but I cannot. Suddenly everything is rushing back—the sight of Maria in the lavish Park Avenue apartment, the sight of Dalia on the gurney, the crazed run that I made through Hermès and the wine shop.

I think Burke senses that I have wandered off to a deeper, darker place. She keeps a steady gaze on me.

Ballard looks confused. He is waiting for me to say something. My tongue freezes as if it's too big for my mouth. My brain is too big for my head, and my heart is too broken to function.

Ballard reaches across the little table and places his rough hand on mine.

"The heart breaks, Detective."

I remain silent. Ballard speaks.

"What can I do, my friend?"

My head is filling with pain. Then I speak.

"Listen to me, Marcel. I believe that someone being held in this prison arranged for the executions of my partner, Maria, and my lover, Dalia. I think whoever it was also planned to kill my current partner, the person sitting here."

I cannot help but notice that Ballard does not react in any way to what I'm saying. He finally removes his hand from mine. He continues to listen silently. If he is anything, he is afraid, stunned.

"It is pure revenge, Ballard. There are men here in Clairvaux who detest me. They don't blame their crimes for their imprisonment. They blame *me*. They think that by killing the people I am close to…they are killing me…and you know something, Ballard? They are right."

Again silence. A long silence. The minute that feels like an hour.

Ballard interrupts the quiet. He is calm. "*C'est vrai, monsieur le lieutenant.* Someone who hates you is killing the women you love."

"Tell me, Marcel. Tell me if you truly have gratitude for what I've done to help your wife and children: do you have any idea who ordered these murders?"

Ballard looks at Burke. Then he looks at me. Then he looks down at the table. When he looks back up again a few moments later his eyes are wet with tears. He speaks.

"Everyone inside this asylum is cruel. You have to learn to be cruel to survive here."

I am awestruck at Ballard's intensity. He continues.

"But there is only one man who has the power to buy such a horror in the outside world. And I think you know who that is. I think you know without my even saying his name."

And I know the person we should bring in.

CHAPTER 43

BURKE AND I WAIT for Adrien Ramus.

We wait in a smaller, bleaker room than the one in which we met with Ballard. This room is located within the high-security area, where the most treacherous prisoners are kept. It is not solitary confinement, but it is the next worst thing. Isolation, only relieved for food and fifteen minutes of recreation a day in the yard.

The room has no table, no chairs. It is bare except for the emergency button, three clubs, and three mace cartridges that hang on the wall.

The door opens with the same horror-film creak as the door in the previous interview room. Tomas Wren once again accompanies the prisoner, but Ramus apparently warrants *three* guards to keep him under control. What's more, I suspect that the handcuffs behind Ramus's back will not be removed.

Ramus is gaunt, thin as a man with a disease. His nose is too big for his face. His eyes are too small for his face. Yet all his characteristics come together to form a frightening but handsome man. He could be an aging fashion model.

Years ago, during his booking, his trials, and his sentencing,

Ramus spat on the floor whenever he saw me. When this vulgarity earned him a club to the head from a policeman or a prison guard, Ramus didn't care. It was worth a little pain to demonstrate his hatred for the detective who had brought him down.

Ramus does not disappoint this time. Upon seeing me he immediately lobs a small puddle of spittle in my direction.

I sense madness—not only in Ramus but also in myself. I reach across and grab him by the chin. I push his head back as far as it will go without snapping it off. I know the guards probably hate Ramus as much as I do. I know they won't stop me. I could beat Ramus if I wished to.

"My partner! My lover!" I shout. "It was you!"

He just stares at me. He twists his neck forcefully, trying to relieve the pain of my assault. I let go of his chin, then shout again.

"You have sources on the outside who can do such things!"

Now Ramus smiles. Then he speaks. The voice is rough, the words staccato.

"You are a fool, Moncrief. I have sources, yes. But anyone inside this pit of hell can buy influence outside. Put the pieces together, Moncrief. Are you so stupid?"

He spits again. Then he just stares at me. I speak more softly now.

"You will burn in hell...and I cannot wait for that time! I cannot wait for God to burn you. And you will do more than die and burn. You will first *suffer*. And then die and burn. I will see to it."

He says, "When I heard that your two women friends were killed I was happy. I was joyful."

My heart is beating hard. My chest is heaving up and down. Ramus continues.

"Some men are very powerful…sometimes even *more* powerful in the shadows of a prison than they are on the streets of the city."

I feel my hand and both my arms tense up completely. In seconds I will be at him once again. This time I will force my hand around his neck. Then I will force my fingers around his Adam's apple. Then…

He speaks again.

"Believe whatever you want, Moncrief. It is of no meaning to me. As I say, you are a stupid, pathetic fool. When will you learn? Where I am concerned, you are powerless. The boss? He is Ramus."

The tension and strength suddenly drain from my body. My arms fall to my side. I am the victim of a perfect crime.

I bow my head. *I have solved the case, but the women closest to me are gone.*

I try to control my shaking limbs. I try to hold my feelings inside me.

"Get him out of here," I say to the guards.

Ramus says nothing more. They lead him out. It's over.

CHAPTER 44

THE NEXT AFTERNOON K. Burke and I fly back to New York City.

Closure. K. Burke is smart enough and now knows me well enough not to talk about "closure," a glib and wishful concept. Nothing closes. At least not completely.

Friends and colleagues and family will say (and some have said already), "You're lucky. At least you're young and rich and handsome. You'll get over this. You'll find a way to learn to move on."

I will nod affirmatively, but only to stop their chatter. Then my response will be simple: "No. Those qualities—youth, wealth, physical attributes—are randomly distributed. They protect you from very little of life's real agonies."

Menashe Boaz and I speak on the telephone. He is still in Norway with his film—"wrapping in three days." His voice, predictably, is somber. I am one of the few people who knows precisely how he feels. With my complete agreement, he decides that he will send two assistants to New York to oversee clearing out Dalia's apartment. Sad? It is beyond sad. Menashe and I cannot have this conversation without the occasional tear. It is a miracle that we can have the conversation at all.

"I don't want a thing from Dalia's apartment," I tell him. I never want to enter the place again.

Any book I've left there I will never finish reading. Any suit in her closet I will never wear again. The real keepsakes are all inside me. A handful of wonderful photographs are on my phone.

Full of jet lag, fatigue, tension, and sorrow, K. Burke and I speak with Inspector Elliott at the precinct. I describe in broad strokes our time in Paris. Burke describes the same thing, but in much greater detail. I say the words I've been aching to say: "The case is solved."

When our two hours with Elliott are over, I tell K. Burke that her memory is "astonishing. I mean it."

She says, "Almost as good as yours. I mean it."

We return to the detective pool—piles of files, the endless recorded phone messages, the crime blotter. I see that Burke is not her usual ambitious self. She is shuffling papers, typing slowly on her computer.

"Something is troubling you, Detective?" I say.

She looks up at me and speaks. "I'm angry that Ramus has brought us down. I know that's stupid. I know the case is solved. But he *has* committed the perfect crime. He can kill and get away with it. It really pisses me off. I can only imagine how you must feel."

"Life goes on, K. Burke. Who knows? Maybe tomorrow will be a little bit better," I say.

Detective Burke smiles. Then she speaks.

"Exactly. Who knows?"

CHAPTER 45

La maison centrale de Clairvaux

ALL PRISONERS ARE EQUAL in the mess hall. At least that's the way it's supposed to be. Same horrid food, same rancid beverages. But in prison, those who have money also have influence. And those with money and influence live a little better.

Marcel Ballard supplies two kitchen workers with a weekly supply of filtered Gauloises cigarettes. So the workers show their gratitude by heaping larger mounds of instant mashed potatoes on Ballard's plate and by giving him a double serving of the awful industrial cheese that is supplied after the meal. On some lucky occasions, Ballard goes to take a slug of water from his tin cup and finds that a kitchen ally has replaced the water with beer or, better still, a good amount of Pernod.

Adrien Ramus has even more influence than Ballard. Ramus, you see, has even more bribery material at his disposal. Even Tomas Wren has snapped at the bait Ramus dangles. Because he gives Wren the occasional gift of a few grams of cocaine, Ramus has a relatively easy time of it in isolation—a private cell, a radio. Ramus sells many things to many prisoners. He always has a supply of marijuana for those who want to get high and access to local attorneys for those who want to get out.

It is Tuesday's supper. The menu never changes. Sunday is a greasy chicken thigh with canned asparagus spears that smell like socks. Monday is spaghetti in a tasteless oil. And then Tuesday. Tuesday at Clairvaux is always—unalterably, predictably—white beans, gray meat in brown gravy, canned spinach, and a thin slice of cheap unidentifiable white cheese.

Guards patrol the aisles.

No conversation is allowed. But that rule is constantly broken, usually with a shout-out declaring, "This food is shit." Sometimes there's a warning from someone just on the edge of sanity, a "Stop staring at me or I'll slice off your balls" or "You are vomiting on me, *gros trou du cul.*" That charming phrase translates as "you big asshole."

This evening is relatively quiet until one man slashes another man's thigh, and as both victim and abuser are hauled away, most of the other prisoners cheer like small stupid boys watching a game. Two other men fight, then they are separated. Two more men fight, and the guards, for their own amusement, allow the fight to proceed for a few minutes until, finally, one man lies semiconscious on the floor.

Suppertime, an allotment of twenty minutes, has almost ended. Some men, like Marcel Ballard, have, for a few euros, bought their neighbor's beans or cheese. Ballard stuffs the food into his round mouth.

Other prisoners have not even touched their plates. Most likely they have chocolate bars and bread hidden in their cells; most likely such luxuries have been supplied—for a price, of course—by Adrien Ramus.

Hundreds of years ago this mess hall was the refectory of Clair-vaux Abbey. Here the hood-clad monks chanted their *"Benedic, Domine,"* the grace said before meals. The faded image of Saint Robert of Molesme, the founder of the Cistercian order, is barely visible above the doors to the kitchen. Often, when some angry prisoner decides to throw a pile of potatoes, the mess ends up on Saint Robert's faded face.

The men are ordered to pass their individual bowls to the end of each table. Most do so quietly. Others find that this chore gives them the opportunity to call a fellow diner a prick or, sometimes more gently, a bitch.

Lukewarm coffee is passed around in tin pitchers. Nothing is ever served hot. Too dangerous. Boiling soup or steaming coffee could be poured over an enemy inmate's head. Almost everyone pours large amounts of sugar into their cups. Almost everyone drinks the coffee, including one of the most prominent and influential prisoners, who sits silently at the end of a table.

That prisoner takes a gulp of coffee. He then places the cup on the wooden table. Suddenly the man's right hand flies to his neck, his left hand to his belly. He lets out a hoarse and stifled gasp. His head begins shaking, and a putrid green liquid surges from his mouth. The prisoners near him move away. Two guards move in on the victim. As trained, two other guards rush to protect the exit doors. This might easily be a scheme to start an uprising.

This, however, turns out not to be a trick. The stricken prisoner falls forward onto the wooden table. His head bounces twice on the wood. His poisoned coffee spills onto the floor. He is dead.

Prisoners are shouting. Guards are swinging their clubs.

Adrien Ramus remains seated. No smile. No anger. No expression. He is satisfied.

At this exact same time, the rest of the world continues turning.

In Paris, a group of French hotel workers are busy replacing the bullet-scarred carpeting where K. Burke was attacked.

In Norway, Menashe Boaz is calling "Cut" and then saying, "Fifteen-minute break." He must be alone.

In New York, Luc Moncrief, who has just come in from running four miles on the West Side bike path, sits in a big leather chair in his apartment. He is sweaty and tired and sad. But for some unknowable reason he finds that he is suddenly at peace.

CHAPTER 46

"I THOUGHT YOU WERE out today," K. Burke says to me, as crisp and confident as ever. Whatever jet-lag body-clock adjustment she had to make has been made.

"I was," I say. "But I had to see you. I must show you something on the computer."

"What's with you, Moncrief? You sound a little—I don't know…creepy. It's like your energy level is down a few notches."

"Yes, Detective. I am stunned. I am walking in a dream. Maybe half a dream and half a nightmare."

As always, about a dozen other New York City detectives are very interested in our conversation. Everyone is aware of the murders. Now many are aware of the attack on Burke in Paris.

"Interview room 4 is free. I checked. Let's go there," I say.

Perhaps for the benefit of our police colleagues, Burke shrugs her shoulders in that I-dunno-maybe-he's-a-little-crazy way. Then she follows me down the hall to the interview room.

I close the curtain to prevent anyone from spying on us through the two-way mirror. I place my laptop on the table, open it, and tap a few buttons.

"I've read it maybe fifty times," I say. "Now it's your turn. Please read. Then I am going to delete it."

K. Burke looks vaguely frightened, but she is also curious. I can tell. Her eyes widen, then they relax. Then her forehead wrinkles. She begins to read.

Monsieur Moncrief:

I believe that the following information will be of interest to you.

Three hours ago, at 1800 hours Paris, an inmate in my charge died, the direct result of poison administered to his coffee.

He was a man of your acquaintance: Marcel Ballard.

Burke looks away from the screen. She looks directly at me. "Ballard?" she says. "But I thought…no. Not Ballard!"

"Keep reading," I say.

Ballard's death was obviously planned and perpetrated by someone inside La maison centrale de Clairvaux.

I know that it was your belief that the murders of Maria Martinez and Dalia Boaz were ordered by another prisoner, Adrien Ramus.

I must inform you, however, that evidence taken here at this scene after today's murder proves otherwise.

An investigation of Ballard's cell revealed a laptop computer hidden within a broken tile beneath the toilet.

An examination of the laptop's contents showed frequent correspondence between Ballard and two Frenchmen who were in the United States on visitor visas. One of them, Thierry Mondeville, returned to France a few days ago. Mondeville has now been identified as the attacker in the incident involving Katherine Burke and yourself.

Further correspondence indicates Ballard's extreme anger at his imprisonment and the role you played in causing it. Ballard explicitly held you responsible for "destroying my life and destroying my family."

Upon its release by the police I will forward a file containing the complete contents of Ballard's computer as well as the findings and conclusions of the official investigation.

> Je vous prie d'agréer, Monsieur, mes
> respectueuses salutations,
> *Tomas Wren*

Burke and I say nothing for a few moments.

Then she looks at me and speaks. "Do you believe this is true?"

I nod, and, for assurance, I say, "I am certain."

I walk to the other side of the room. I look out the perpetually dirty window. The tops of the brownstones look like figures drawn in charcoal when seen through the dirt on the glass.

"But, Moncrief, you mean…all these years you were helping Ballard, and all these years he was planning to destroy your life?" she says. "You must be amazed at this."

"To be honest, I am not amazed. *I knew.*"

Now Burke is the one who is amazed. She is speechless.

"Ramus is indeed a wretched excuse for a human being. But if he had ordered the executions he would have happily bragged to me about them. He would have told me directly that he was the talent behind the killings. But…he stopped just short of bragging.

"That is why I assaulted him. But I could not drive him to say what he would have been glad to say. He would not admit to being the force behind the killings.

"Then we add the fact that Ballard was so effusive in his thanks to me. Bah! I put him in prison for most of his life. Do you think he cares what happens to his family? Do you think he cares about their welfare? I instinctively knew he was throwing the *connerie,* the bullshit, at me."

I can tell she wants to smile, but this moment is too serious.

"But most important, *I could not have put Ramus in prison if Ballard had not given me information on him.* I knew that some-day Ramus would punish Ballard. This was timing *parfait.* Ballard falsely pinned the crimes on Ramus *and* Ballard had previously be-trayed him. So, *le poison dans le café.*"

"So the case is solved," she says. But she speaks softly, cautiously.

"I guess so," I say. I know, however, that there is sorrow in my voice.

I walk back to the table where the opened laptop rests. Then I push the button marked DELETE.

CHAPTER 47

I LEAVE THE PRECINCT and head toward Fifth Avenue and 52nd Street. I am standing outside a fabulous shop, Versace. I pause and then walk through the great arched center door.

This was one of Dalia's favorite stores. I can remember almost every single item Dalia ever bought here.

The black skirt. If I looked hard I could see through the tightly woven material and catch a glimpse of Dalia's exquisite legs.

The shoes with thick cork platforms that made Dalia a half inch or so taller than I am. We always laughed at that.

The belts with golden buckles. The black leather shopping totes. The crazy shirts with variously colored geometric shapes that shout at you.

"Signor Moncrief. It has been a thousand years since we have seen you," says the store manager, Giuliana. "Welcome. You have been away, perhaps?" she adds.

"Yes. I've been away. Far away."

Giuliana tilts her head to one side. "I heard of the tragedy of Miss Boaz, of course. We were all so sad."

"Thank you," I say. "I read your condolence note. I read it more than once."

"We liked her so very much," says Giuliana. Then she says, "I will leave you alone. Call on me if I can help you."

"I will," I say. *"Grazie."*

She walks away, and I remain still, moving only my head. I take in the lights from the golden fixtures. The multitude of wallets laid out in their cases in neat overlapping rows.

It is late summer. So they are showing fall coats, fall dresses, fall scarves. Reds and browns and dark yellows. Black jeans and white jeans. And lots and lots of sunglasses. Even the mannequins are wearing sunglasses.

"Sunglasses are always in season," Dalia used to say.

I am about to move deeper into the store. I am calm. Not completely calm, but I am calm.

Then my phone rings. The caller is identified as "K. Burke."

I answer.

"Good afternoon, K. Burke. Don't tell me. There's been a murder."

"How did you know?" she says.

"I just knew. Somehow I just knew."

ABOUT THE AUTHORS

JAMES PATTERSON has written more bestsellers and created more enduring fictional characters than any other novelist writing today. He lives in Florida with his family.

RICHARD DiLALLO is a former advertising creative director. He has had numerous articles published in major magazines. He lives in Manhattan with his wife.

HAVE YOURSELF A SCARY LITTLE CHRISTMAS.

In the heart of the holiday season, priceless paintings have vanished from a Park Avenue murder scene. Now, dashing French detective Luc Moncrief must become a quick study in the art of the steal—before a cold-blooded killer paints the town red.

Merry Christmas, Detective.

THE CHRISTMAS MYSTERY
A DETECTIVE LUC MONCRIEF
STORY

JAMES PATTERSON
WITH RICHARD DiLALLO

Read the thrilling holiday whodunit *The Christmas Mystery,* coming soon only from

BOOKSHOTS

EAT, DRINK, AND BE MURDERED.

Someone is poisoning the diners in New Orleans' best
restaurants. Now it's up to chef and homicide cop Caleb Rooney
to catch a killer set on revenge—a dish best served cold.

KILLER CHEF

JAMES PATTERSON
WITH JEFFREY J. KEYES

**Read the delicious new mystery *Killer Chef*,
coming soon from**

BOOKSHOTS

MICHAEL BENNETT FACES HIS TOUGHEST CASE YET....

Detective Michael Bennett is called to the scene after a
man plunges to his death outside a trendy Manhattan hotel—but
the man's fingerprints are traced to a pilot who was
killed in Iraq years ago.

Will Bennett discover the truth?

Or will he become tangled in a web of government secrets?

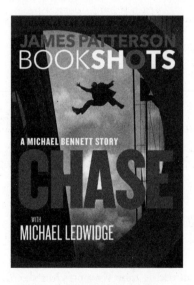

**Read the new action-packed Michael Bennett story, *Chase,*
available now only from**

BOOKSHOTS

"I'M NOT ON TRIAL. SAN FRANCISCO IS."

Drug cartel boss the Kingfisher has a reputation for being violent and merciless. And after he's finally caught, he's set to stand trial for his vicious crimes—until he begins unleashing chaos and terror upon the lawyers, jurors, and police associated with the case. The city is paralyzed, and Detective Lindsay Boxer is caught in the eye of the storm.

Will the Women's Murder Club make it out alive—or will a sudden courtroom snare ensure their last breaths?

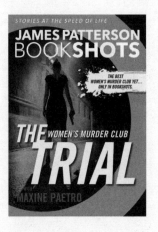

Read the shocking new Women's Murder Club story, available now only from

BOOKSHOTS

Looking to Fall in Love in Just One Night?

Introducing BookShots Flames:

Original romances presented by James Patterson that fit into your busy life.

Featuring Love Stories by:

New York Times bestselling author Jen McLaughlin

New York Times bestselling author Samantha Towle

USA Today bestselling author Erin Knightley

Elizabeth Hayley

Jessica Linden

Codi Gary

Laurie Horowitz

…and many others!

Available only from

James Patterson's
BOOKSH⊕TS
Flames

HER SECOND CHANCE AT LOVE MIGHT BE TOO GOOD TO BE TRUE....

When Chelsea O'Kane escapes to her family's inn in Maine, all she's got are fresh bruises, a gun in her lap, and a desire to start anew. That's when she runs into her old flame, Jeremy Holland. As he helps her fix up the inn, they rediscover what they once loved about each other.

Until it seems too good to last...

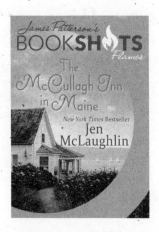

Read the stirring story of hope and redemption
The McCullagh Inn in Maine, **available now from**